Battle of

Anne Fine

First published in 2016 by Endeavour Press Ltd.

Table of Contents

A Glimpse into the Future...

Tory heard nothing. Still, Archie was going crazy, standing full square and barking at the letterbox. Already on her way across the hall, Tory took hold of his collar and hushed him sharply. Then she opened the door.

On the step lay a package. It was tallish, rectangular and wrapped none too neatly in crumpled brown paper. Tory looked round but no one was about – no, not in the darkened garden, nor passing beneath the street lamps further along Staines Crescent. Whoever delivered the box must have scuttled away very quickly.

She waited, half expecting to hear a car start up, but all was quiet outside. The only sounds were Archie's keen sniffing at the package and the soft burble behind from the television Barry was watching.

Tory scooped up the package and carried it into the kitchen. Even before she'd pulled off the wrapping, Barry was in the doorway. 'What's that, then?'

'I thought it might be flowers,' Tory admitted. 'But it's too heavy for that.'

He grinned. 'Got an admirer, have you?'

Tory ignored him. The last of the brown wrapping fell away, exposing a cheap wooden box. Lifting the lid, she reached inside to pull out a cream-coloured plastic urn.

'What the hell?' Barry had stepped in front of Tory to swivel the urn round and read the handwritten label stuck to its side.

Presumed Cremated Remains, Identity Unknown, Recovered from Childon Cemetery.

'Oh, really!' Tory said. '"Identity unknown"! How childish can they get?'

'It beggars belief,' agreed Barry. 'Do you suppose they actually got down on their hands and knees and scraped his ashes out of the grave?'

'With the vicar standing watching.'

'Glancing at her watch.'

'Murmuring something about hating to mention it, but being just a teensy bit pressed for time.'

'Another burial… You know how it goes…'

Barry raised the urn to shake it, then unscrewed the plastic lid to peer in. 'Not much inside.'

'There wouldn't have been much of him to put inside. Each of us only threw a tiny bit.'

Suddenly Barry was reaching behind him for the newspaper and spreading it flat on the table.

'Barry, no!'

But he had done it. He had tipped out the contents of the urn. 'So that's the last of your stepdad, then.'

'Yes,' Tory said forlornly. 'That's the last of my stepdad.'

Both of them burst out laughing.

Part 1

1.

Maybe, thought Tory, they had never taken the whole thing seriously enough. It was so long since Megan first raised the issue. She'd drummed her fingers on the bistro table just enough to make it clear to Tory that she thought the conversation they were having was a waste of time. Tory teased on for a while, merrily chatting about why she had left her last workplace, complaining about Barry's recent brutalist haircut, admiring her sister's new scarf.

But finally she'd cracked. 'Is something on your mind?'

Megan had taken to making a fan of her napkin. 'No. Not at all. Well actually, yes.'

'A problem?'

'I think so. And so does Malcolm.'

Tory took great care not to let her irritation show. 'Oh, well!' she wanted to say, 'If Malcolm thinks there's a problem...' But it was not safe to tease Megan that way. To Megan, Malcolm was to be respected as a fount of knowledge and the avatar of perfect judgement. ('You wouldn't believe what our investments earned last year,' she'd once said in a rather tactless moment – although the figure would have been impossible for Tory to credit in any case, given that Megan was just discreet enough not to say the amount aloud.)

'Is it about Mum?'

Mum was, after all, still lying in the nearby hospital after her third operation. Suddenly Tory's spirits rose. Perhaps the two of them, her sister and brother-in-law, had come to their senses at last and realised it was time to stop encouraging Elinor to keep letting surgeons chase the cancer that was killing her. Was Megan about to say, 'We think that maybe she should give up on all these operations and chemotherapy and stuff, and just try to enjoy her last few months.'?

No such luck.

'Actually, it's about her will.'

'Her will?'

'And Gordon's.' Since Tory's face stayed blank, Megan said impatiently, 'You do know what's in them?'

'Well, no. Not really. I mean, I do know that we two are down as executors.'

'Only of Mum's,' said Megan. 'If you remember, Gordon preferred to use his own solicitor and the son of a friend.'

She made it sound as if the choice still rankled. Pretending not to notice her sister's resentful tone, Tory said mildly, 'I don't believe I've ever read the wills. Are they unhinged, or something? Will both of them be leaving all their loot to a cats' home?' She grinned. 'Or, worse, to just one cat?'

'Of course not!' Megan was clearly not in the mood for levity. 'It's just that they're not fair.'

Oh, God. Not fair. That pitiful childhood bleat. Small wonder Barry called his sister-in-law Misery Meg. But Tory made an effort. 'I thought they each plan to leave everything they have to one another. That's what Gordon told me. That's fair, isn't it? They have been married thirty years.'

'Twenty-eight.'

Long enough not to quibble, anyway. But that was Megan all over. She'd never taken to Gordon Forsyth. Right from the start she'd acted as if their widowed mother's decision, first to go out with him, then to stay in, and in the end to marry, was one long sorry mistake. The rest of them had tried to ignore the sulks, and hope that Megan's chilly patches would soon blow over. And after a while her festering resentment had seemed to lessen. But still it sprang up at odd moments to upset their mother and unnerve them all, sometimes in an ungracious response: 'Oh, is this gift from both of you? I hadn't realised. Sorry.' Or in affected astonishment: 'But why would Gordon want to come to my prize-giving? He's not my father.'

Bad age to lose your real dad, though, at eight years old. And Megan had been the apple of their father's eye, or so they told themselves when they were trying to downplay the mardy moods she fell in, and the person she became.

Tory picked up her fork. 'All right, then. Twenty-eight years. That's still a long time to be married. And I can't see what else you would expect.'

Her sister waved this contribution to the conversation aside. 'That's not the issue. The problem is that it's down in both wills that, on the second death, each of the grandchildren will get a lump sum, and what's left after that will be divided between the two of us.'

'Yes?'

'But don't you see? It isn't fair. You've got three children and we only have two.'

Tory looked down at her large pasta squares. It was so hard to even like her sister, let alone love her. What was the best thing to say? In the end, all she could manage was, 'I think that Gordon and Elinor probably thought they'd like to set all five grandchildren up a bit in life. After all, everyone that age needs a financial boost. The whole world thinks that way. You must have read about it in the papers. "The Bank of Mum and Dad." People are on about it all the time.'

'That's not the point.'

Tory bisected her pasta. 'So what is the point? Should Barry and I have not had Ned, simply to keep the will bequests even-stevens with you and Malcolm?' She raised her head to look her sister in the eye. 'Perhaps you think we should have had an abortion?'

Her sister shrank – not at the insult, Tory realised, but at the realisation that the ugly word had been heard by the couple at the next table. Rallying almost at once, Megan said, 'Don't be ridiculous, Tory. I only think the same amount of money should be put aside for each set of grandchildren. Our half would be split between Bethany and Amy, and yours would have to be divided between your three. After all, it was your choice to have a bigger family. The way things are at present, after the grandchildren have all had their bequests, Malcolm and I will end up with a good deal less than our fair share. And that's not equitable, is it?'

Equitable. That was a Malcolm word if ever there was one. Tory laid down her fork. Right. Megan had asked for it. Now she was going to get it.

She smiled seraphically. 'I really wouldn't worry about it,' she told her sister. 'Not for a moment. Mum might be on her way out, but Gordon is in the pink. He's obviously going to last for years. How long did his parents live? Till they were well into their nineties, both of them. And by the time it comes round to it, we'll find that walking frames and private carers and nursing homes and round-the-clock laundry and all that stuff costs the earth. By the time Gordon pops his clogs, every last penny will have gone, and all our two families will be divvying up is some dribbled-on shirts and a few pairs of pee-stained trousers.' She raised her glass to Megan in a mocking toast. 'And honestly, you will be welcome to your exact fair share of those.'

Dare she go further? Dare she add, 'Your equitable share.'?

No. Better stop. Already Megan was signalling to the barista. Usually these little verbal spats were fine, usefully serving to remind each sister not to make any arrangement to meet again too soon. But now, with Mum in hospital, avoiding one another was not an option and Tory realised she had been stupid to indulge herself.

Desperately she tried to backtrack. 'Must you be off? No pud or anything?'

'No, thanks. But very kind indeed of you to offer.'

Terrific sarcasm! For Tory never paid the bill when they were at Ben's Bistro. She always hinted they should meet at Sweet Delights, where they could have a far, far cheaper cake and coffee instead. It was Megan who, from time to time, insisted on making lunch her treat – and who, although she stuck to tap water from the carafe, encouraged her sister to have a glass or two of wine. Tory considered putting up a fight: 'No. Let me get it this time.' But Megan would never let her win, not after that attack. And even if she had passed the bill over the table simply out of spite, Tory would have had to nip out to the nearest machine to get more cash. She couldn't put another penny on the credit card. Barry would kill her.

She tried another way of crawling back into her sister's good books. 'You're right. Best not even to look at the desserts. I've got so fat since all this hospital business began. I just sit by Mum's bed and eat.'

'A pity Mum can't join you,' Megan snapped.

Honours were even. Outside, the pair of them managed the usual parting embrace, laced with the usual relief. Tory refused her sister's unenthusiastic offer of a ride home. 'No, honestly, I have a couple of things round here I must get done. And I'm fine with the bus. They come every few minutes.'

She waited till Megan had fished out her car keys and vanished round the corner. Then she strode to the unprotected bus stop, and there she waited half an hour in a chill wind, quietly hating her sister.

Megan drove home in a fury. She had to make an effort not to tailgate all the ditherers, or sound her horn the moment the lights turned green. Almost the only thing that kept her in check was being so aware of what the rest of the world thought of the people who drove cars like hers. (Arrogant. Arsy. Inconsiderate. Up themselves.)

And yet she'd earned this silver beauty – every last inch of its lush, gleaming bodywork, each carefully oiled component of its high-powered engine. (She presumed engines were still oiled.) All of those years of getting by on nothing, stuffing envelopes late into the night and never going out. But finally, as Malcolm prophesied, the firm had reached a tipping point. Money began to flow in a good deal faster than it flowed out. The girls were moved from the local school into the more salubrious St Hilda's. Megan hired a cleaning lady, then doubled the number of her hours. Then doubled them again.

And they were made.

So how dare Tory look at her with such contempt, implying that she'd been petty to raise the topic of their stepfather's will? How things would fall out can't have been what anyone intended. Tory's Ned was an accident, born more than two years after the will was made. A full seven years after his sister Lindy. Six years after Lou.

Lindy! Lou! Her nieces' very names got on her nerves. Even on their respective birth certificates Barry had opted for these casual versions of two otherwise sensible names. Megan could remember her brother-in-law chuckling as he said it: 'If it's another daughter, we're going to call her Louisa. Then I can save time when I want both of them, just calling "Lindy-Lou".'

'Why not just call her Lou?' Tory had said, clutching her massive belly.

And so they had! But children's names were not a joke, like the one Malcolm made on that journey years ago. He'd suddenly claimed he'd love to buy some dismal house in Turvey. 'But it's so horrible!' Megan had said as they drove past the battered *For Sale* sign. 'Ugly as sin, and right on the main road.'

He'd chuckled. 'But this is Bedfordshire. And it's called "Topsy". Get the joke, Megan? We'd have the best address ever. We'd live in Topsy, Turvey, Beds.'

See? Just a stupid fancy – something whimsical to say on a tiresome car journey. Not something you would ever do.

And that was just a house, not a real child.

But they had always been like that, Tory and Barry. So sure that all their little foibles and amusements were not just acceptable to other people, but actually admired. They probably lay in bed at night after one of their mad parties or grotty, spur-of-the-moment, grubby-forked suppers for friends, and thought that all their guests were climbing into their own beds, saying wistfully, 'They're such an interesting couple.'

Well, she and Malcolm didn't think that way. What was so interesting about being so broke that you could only offer other people great heaps of pasta in a rather nasty sauce? Or one of those frightful bean stews. What was so interesting about being so taken up with your own life that you didn't bother to check your children's homework? Ever! Or even read between the lines at parents' evenings? Didn't Tory and Barry realise that 'oh, Lou's a lovely girl – a pleasure to have in the class' meant no more than 'she sits there quietly and is no trouble'. It didn't mean that Lou was working. Or even that she was set fair to pass her exams. You have to push a teacher far, far harder than that to find out what is really going on.

Just look at Lindy. Pretty well at the end of her school career with singularly little to show for it. A few pathetic grades in a few easy subjects. Nothing to get the poor child anywhere in life. And Lou and Ned were headed the same way. Megan wouldn't forget the time she'd driven Elinor to Tory's after their mother had broken her ankle. Tory had waved the two of them into the living room. She must have seen Ned sprawled across the floor, his eyes glued to something manic on a screen. But she'd said nothing. It was up to Megan to say to her nephew sharply, 'Can you please move. Your granny here is on crutches.'

There again, Tory and Barry had always been what they called 'laissez-faire', making a joke of almost everything to do with raising children. Even when Ned was small they'd let him sit in front of rubbish for hours on end. The child would just pretend he hadn't heard any request for him to switch things off, or down. Once Megan had gone round with a cardboard box filled with expensive dog food. (Bonnie had been put down, and since the girls had lost all interest in pets, there didn't seem a reason to replace her.)

'Good stuff!' said Barry, reading the various labels on the tins. 'A real treat for Archie. All the poor fellow usually gets is that dried rubbish.' Then he inspected the empty box. 'This will be useful too.'

She had been mystified when he picked up a Stanley knife. (And what was that doing lying about at table height? Ned was just four.) The kettle was left boiling frantically as Barry carved a square out of the carton's side.

'Does your kettle not switch off automatically?' Megan had asked him anxiously after a while.

He shrugged. 'Sometimes.'

Ignoring the continuing blast of steam against the blistered cabinet, he'd set himself to drawing function keys under his cut-out square. 'There. This might work.'

'But what's it for?'

'Ned. He only ever pays attention to things on screens.'

Dropping the box over his head, Barry had marched through to the living room. 'Here is a public service announcement,' he declared through the hacked-out rectangle. 'Turn down the bloody sound!'

Megan had not been able to stop herself. 'Barry! You mustn't use that sort of language in front of Ned!'

'Oh, Ned's heard worse.'

'That's not the point!' With shredded nerves, she had slid off her stool to switch off the kettle at the plug. 'He'll start to speak like that at school and be excluded.'

'It worked, though, didn't it?' said Barry, coming back into the kitchen.

To her chagrin she realised that the blaring of the dinosaurs had softened to some background grunts. Knowing she'd be incapable of saying nothing more about the dangers of a kettle boiling dry, she had reached for her coat and hurried off.

She hated visiting their house. She hated them.

*

Barry had quite forgotten that Tory had lunched with her sister. He only realised when she raised the lid of the pan that was hissing away on the stove top and told him, 'Good thing I like pasta so much.'

'Is that what you had at the bistro?'

'Yes. But that was different.' She peered at the sauce again. 'Will there be enough?'

'The kids ate earlier. Lou and Ned claimed to be starving and Lindy was off to Jade's.'

'Overnight?'

'I suppose so.'

'Didn't she say?'

'I'm sure she'll ring.' He slid a couple of plates along the table. 'So what did Megan want?'

Tory lifted the pan and carried it to the table. She put it down on the worst scorch ring as if it doubled as a protective mat. 'How do you know she wanted anything at all?'

He tipped the pasta into the colander. 'Because she made the date. These days she must bump into you practically every other evening at the hospital. Why would she want to talk to you somewhere else, unless there was something that she wanted to say?'

'You're cunning, you are.' Tory tapped the side of her nose. 'You suss out everything.'

He grinned. 'So tell me. What was it? Have they decided to stop encouraging your poor old mum to think she's immortal?'

'No,' Tory said. 'It's just the usual.'

'Another gripe? What is it this time?'

'The wills. Megan and Malcolm reckon that they're—'

Barry was forced to wait while, fork aloft, his wife did a memory search. 'Inequitable.'

'Inequitable?'

'The loot they'll be leaving the kids. We have three children and they only have two, so it's not fair.'

Now it was Barry's turn to leave his cutlery hovering in mid-air. 'I don't believe it! That house is made of money. They all drip with it. What is she doing fussing about something as petty as that?'

Tory shrugged. 'Everyone knows that people don't get rich by accident. And they don't stay rich by taking anything to do with money lightly. Remember Miss Tallentire's cow byre?'

'Oh, God! The cow byre! We had a good few chuckles about that.'

Indeed they had. Miss Tallentire had owned the cow byre for over sixty years. Its slates were slipping and the guttering hung uselessly over

16

clogged drains. Almost as soon as Malcolm and Megan had built their brand new house on what was once Miss Tallentire's paddock, Malcolm had offered to buy it. ('It would be useful for storing our lawnmower. And it will save you from the trouble of repairs.') Miss Tallentire wasn't daft. She had called someone in to look the cow byre over and tell her what she ought to ask, and she and Malcolm had agreed on not much less than that, and on shared costs. But what she hadn't known was that her helpful new neighbour was all too pally with the solicitor he'd vaguely suggested they might use to draw up the paperwork.

Tory had overheard the two of them plotting. Taking a break at Megan and Malcolm's rather stiff housewarming party, she'd listened from behind a door.

'A stone shed sort of thing? A simple enough transfer generally. Shouldn't cost much.'

'There was a right of way across Miss Tallentire's yard.'

'I suppose I could make something out of that. Whip up a few small complications…'

'Yes, that would help. Go towards covering part of the costs of my new workshop deal, maybe?'

'Yes, that one is going to work out rather pricey, I'm afraid.'

'Well, see what you can do. It's not as if the old lady's on her last bean.'

Tory reported the conversation on the drive home. Barry began by taking a generous view. 'It can't be what you think.'

'It can. The world is full of sleazy solicitors.'

'You truly think that Malcolm's getting his mate to tweak the bills so poor Miss Tallentire ends up paying a hefty chunk of one of his other deals?'

'That's what it sounded like.'

'So are you going to tackle Malcolm?'

'Hell, no. Are you?'

'You're joking!'

Yet the two of them had thought of something. Barry had worn the very passable beard he'd just been given for the dress rehearsal of *The Pirate King*. And in her best secretary's voice, Tory had rung Miss Tallentire. 'I'm sending our Mr Harris round to see you. There are a couple of things he wants to make quite clear before you formally agree this cow byre deal.'

Barry had shown up later that day, trusting that Miss Tallentire's eighty-year-old eyesight would pick up nothing odd about the beard. She'd given him a quizzical look. Her lips had even primped into a smile. But she'd invited him to take a seat. 'The thing is,' he had said after a couple of civilities, 'you must insist your equal contribution to the legal fees is capped at something really sensible.' He'd named the price that someone he knew from walks with Archie had claimed should cover such a transfer deal. 'And even that, of course, must be inclusive of value added tax and all other disbursements.'

Miss Tallentire gave him a somewhat baffled look, but she had nodded.

'That's good, then,' Barry said. 'I'll get my secretary to sort things out.'

He fled. And Tory made the call to Malcolm's man, James Harrow. 'I'm phoning on behalf of Miss Tallentire. She isn't sure she made it absolutely clear that...'

Barry was waggling the beard at her. How she got to the end without a giggle she'd never know. But it had foiled Malcolm. The few small 'complications' melted away before the deal was done.

'That was a laugh,' Tory said now.

'And a warning.' He eased a second dollop of the pasta out of the pan. 'What do you think the two of them will do?'

'With Mum knocking at Death's door? Nothing yet, I should think. There isn't any point. Mum's share goes straight to Gordon and, right now, Gordon's as fit as a lop.'

2.

Gordon Forsyth died that night. Nothing traumatic, it seemed, for when the cleaning lady found him in bed next morning, she thought for quite a while he was asleep.

'I just presumed he was worn out from all this to-ing and fro-ing with the hospital. I know from visiting my own mum that you can wait forever for that lift. I told him several times, "You'd best be patient, Mr Forsyth. You're no spring chicken yourself." But he just said that stairs were good for people.' Mrs Deloy looked down at the body again. 'Who would have thought it, though? What with your poor mother being in such a bad way herself.'

'Nobody would have thought it,' said Megan. She wished that Mrs Deloy, rather than wallowing in the morning's excitement, would do as she'd been asked – put all her cleaning stuff away and leave the house. There were so many phone calls to be made, and Malcolm was out of town. She had rung Tory's landline several times, only to get no answer – and no means to leave a message. (How did they live like that when they had teenage children?) She'd phoned her sister's mobile, though she knew that Tory made a point of never bothering to take it anywhere. 'I can't stand being tracked about the planet. It's unnatural.'

She'd never even known her brother-in-law's mobile number. So there was nothing for it. She would have to phone him at work.

She got the sort of run-around she was expecting. 'I'm sorry. Mr Challoner is dealing with a client now. Could you ring back in the lunch hour?'

'I need to find his wife,' said Megan. 'I need to tell her that our stepfather's dead.'

That shook the girl into action. 'Hang on.' She heard a door open and close, and in the background the soft chattering of some sort of machine. She waited, resting the side of her head against the door frame. She was exhausted. What was it Macbeth said about his wife? 'She should have died hereafter. There would have been a time for such a word.'

That's how she felt – that Gordon might almost have picked his moment just to annoy her. Not that she wished him ill. She recognised that he had done his level best to be a decent stepfather. He had been patient with her. He'd put up with a goodly number of her mardy moods, And never once rebuked her.

But she had loved her dad. Her real dad. She had adored him, in fact. She'd been his shadow as a child. She'd learned the name of almost everything they sold in the nearby plant nursery because he gardened. She'd probably only studied languages at university because he'd once said he regretted fooling about so much in French lessons when he was back at school. She had been devastated when he was killed in that stupid car crash. For years she'd fantasised that she'd track down the thuggy young drunk driver and slide a knife between his ribs, or run him down. And she'd talked to her father every night. That's why she'd made that fuss to keep a bedroom of her own even though little Tory had got herself in such a state about snakes under the bed. Megan had needed to feel free to have those endless made-up conversations with her dad under the bedclothes. She might have gone around with black rings round her eyes, but talking half the night with her dead father had been the only thing that kept her from screaming till her throat tore.

So Gordon had been nothing to her. Nothing. Tory had come to terms with him quite soon – competing with him on computer games, telling him gossip from school and sharing jokes. To Megan, he remained simply the man who sat across the table at meals, drove her to school, and went with them on foreign holidays.

She had come round, of course, soon after she herself was married. She'd come to realise just how awkward life would have been if Mum had not had Gordon to keep her busy. Especially after Bethany was born. If Elinor had still been living alone, she would have shown up at their house on one grandmotherly excuse after another, disrupting their work schedules and disapproving of the hours Bethany had spent in nursery. No, Gordon had been a good thing, and Megan had been prepared to meet her obligations. She'd even thought of bringing him to live with them after Mum died – first in their stylish guest annexe, but with a view to snapping up Miss Tallentire's cottage as soon as it went on the market. All it would need was better dry-walling and a proper makeover.

This could not have been a worse week for one more thing to happen.

How could she think that way! How could somebody's death be 'one more thing'? And yet it was. Megan was stretched to the limit and beyond. Amy was taking her Grade eight violin examination tomorrow, and piano on Thursday. Both times she would need driving to the music school in Bramley. Bethany, too, had serious school tests this week, and would be panicking. On top of that there were a host of printing deadlines she and Malcolm could not ignore – not if they aimed to keep the clients. And Malcolm's car was in the garage.

Bummer, as Tory would say (in front of Ned, no doubt).

At last she heard the office girl's voice come back near the telephone. 'It's that one, Mr Challoner.' And he picked up. 'Megan? Are you there?'

To her astonishment, she felt tears rolling down her cheeks.

'Megan? Is that you?'

She could tell from his voice that he'd been told. 'Barry, I am so sorry to interrupt.'

'No, no.' She almost saw him wave away the client he'd abandoned. 'Don't worry about that. What's going on? Is Gordon—? I mean, can it be true? Has he—?'

She nodded, hardly realising how stupid that was, then said, 'Yes. So I need Tory. He's just lying here, and there's so much to do, and—'

She stopped, distracted by the taste of tears.

He asked her, 'Has the doctor showed up yet?'

'Doctor?' She felt a surge of irritation. 'Gordon is dead.'

'But you still need a doctor.'

Of course she did. She knew that. 'I know that!'

'You phone a doctor,' he told her. 'Do that now. Whoever comes will tell you what to do. And I will do my level best to track down Tory.'

His level best? Exasperation shook her. What sort of marriage is it when you can't be confident that you can find your other half? All this 'free spirit' nonsense! Suppose it was Ned who'd had some accident and died? Suppose it was Lindy or Lou? She was infuriating, Tory. Never around when she was needed. She would have swanned off somewhere hip and grubby to do her tantric meditation, or exercises on her silly yoga mat. Walking the hills, maybe. 'Oh, I had such a magic day. I never saw a soul from one hill's end to the next.'

As irresponsible as ever. Stupid cow.

Tory was on a bed at Bramley Turkish Baths, pretending to be foreign. Whenever another woman said something friendly from a nearby bed, or as she passed, Tory would shrug forlornly and mutter a few guttural words – 'Tak mentak blett,' or some such. Since no one paying to relax likes the idea of struggling through a conversation with a foreigner, it worked a treat – except, of course, for that time when she'd failed to recognise an old school friend of Barry's, and had to pretend that she'd been saying, 'Hi! How's tricks?' in fluent Albanian for a joke.

For Tory, though, relaxing had been proving difficult. She couldn't help it, she was thinking about Lindy and Lou. Lindy was going nowhere – except out, of course. Practically every night. Ask her where she was going and you got your head snapped off. Give her a time to come home and she'd ignore it (not that they'd tried that often since Lindy turned sixteen). She never seemed to tackle any homework. She never seemed to read anything beyond those stupid series on teenage passions or handsome vampires. (Those she read over and over, no doubt using the heroes as templates for her sexy dreams.)

And Lou was headed the same way, without the pouting and sulks. (So far.) All clothes and hair and shopping and me, me, me. And always wanting things. Neither girl ever so much as glanced at a newspaper unless the headline was the sort to grab the attention of the undead: *WOMAN CHEWS OFF OWN ARM AFTER ROCK FALL* or *MAN BOILS WIFE'S SAWN-OFF HEAD TO MUSH*. That sort of thing.

Perhaps she and Barry should have done what Megan and Malcolm did, and moved their daughters to a different school. Somewhere a bit more ambitious. But Lindy and Lou had both been happy where they were, and all the teachers said nice things about them. 'Very helpful girls.' 'Always a pleasure to teach.'

But they'd been worried none the less, especially when Lindy came home and talked about what they'd been doing in biology. It was the sort of stuff that she and Barry learned in primary school. She'd tried to shrug it off. Times change, and you can always look things up online. Still, it had bothered her. And the sheer lack of actual grammar in the French books they brought home almost made her hair curl. Barry knew more than that, and he had dropped French at the very first chance.

Yes, they should probably have moved the girls – begged Mum and Gordon to loan them money to pay the fees, or scrubbed around for some sort of scholarships. Given up foreign holidays. Done what it takes. Except that Megan had come round one evening simply to tick them off. Literally tick them off! 'I don't know what you think is going to happen,' she'd said. 'That school is quite notorious for letting children coast. It's had the same weak head teacher for five years now. The turnover in staff has always been appalling, but now the catchment area is widening to take in the Fairley Estate, it'll get worse.'

Tory had glanced across the table to see Barry rolling his eyes. 'Oh, come on, Megan. It's really good for children to meet all sorts. Your girls will end up all the poorer for not knowing how to mix with other people.'

God, she'd turned snitty. 'There's a good social mix at St Hilda's. It's just that they all have one thing in common, and that is parents who understand the importance of education.' She'd leaned across the table, wagging her finger at Tory. 'You and I went to good schools ourselves. You know we did. So how can you ignore the fact that Lindy and Lou are just being taught to the most basic standard. Pretty well the only children who fly in that school are ones whose parents buy them extra tutoring.'

'That isn't true.'

'It's a huge place. There must be several hundred pupils there. And hardly any of them go on to good universities.'

'What makes a university "good", Megan?' Barry had asked her with a scornful look. And Megan had mercifully shut up because she knew she'd lost the battle and she'd gone too far. Far too far. After that evening, Barry and Tory would probably have boiled their daughters in oil rather than follow her advice and take them out of Mansfield School. Oh, they had justified it to themselves on any number of grounds. But Tory knew that the decision mostly stemmed from stubbornness. There were a few short weeks when she and Barry brimmed with ideas about how to enrich their children's education without switching schools: plays, concerts, visits to museums and private music lessons. All of them perfectly possible, but all of them a deal of money or a slog. Who wanted to end up like Megan and Malcolm anyway, forever chauffeuring their girls from one enriching pastime to another? And what was so important about an enhanced curriculum? Wasn't it equally important just to be happy?

Tory heard footsteps and felt a shadow on her face. Opening her eyes she saw a friendly-looking person standing over her.

'Tak mentak blett,' said Tory automatically.

'Mrs Challoner? We have a phone call for you at the desk. It is your husband and he says it's urgent.'

*

'Barry? How did you know that I was here?'

'I didn't. I think I must have phoned every damn place you've ever been. Now listen, Tory. Something has happened. Gordon is dead.'

'Gordon?'

'Yes.'

'Dead? Really?'

'So it seems. Mrs Deloy came in to do her stuff. Apparently she hoovered round him for a while until the penny dropped. Then she phoned Megan.'

'My God! Poor Gordon! Dead. Blimey! So what's happening now?'

'I think Megan's dealing with the doctor and the death certificate. And I expect she'll have an undertaker's firm in mind because of that last fright with your mum.'

'Oh, Christ! Mum! Does she know?'

'I shouldn't think so. Even your sister isn't quite as officious as that.'

'Officious? Mum will have to be told.'

'I just meant Megan will probably have the grace to hold back telling Elinor until she's spoken to you.' She heard him sigh. 'You know. In case the two of you want to do it together.'

Her recent thoughts had clearly not been good for Tory. 'Sisters and all that, do you mean?'

'I suppose so.'

'Is that the form, then?'

Now he was slightly tart of tongue himself. 'How would I know?'

He wouldn't, Tory realised. His parents had died years and years ago. 'No, no. You're right. I'd better go to the house now. She'll want to talk to me. Tell me what's what.'

'Give you your marching orders, so to speak.'

'That sort of thing.'

'Tory,' he said, before she could hang up. 'It has sunk in?'

'Yes, yes. Well, it is sinking.'

'I'll let her know you're on your way. And you be careful,' he reminded her. She knew that, if they hadn't had to sell the second car, he would have said, 'Drive carefully.'

She made a joke of it. 'I'll look both ways before I cross the road.'

It merited a taxi. But there were none about, and then the bus came. On the ride back she thought about her stepfather. He'd been a really nice man, endlessly patient with her and Megan, even when Megan was a pain. He'd done most of the ferrying about when they were young, and later he had covered for her more than once when she'd told fibs about where she had been or what she'd done. He had a gift for making sensible decisions, and getting others to agree with him without being overbearing. Why, it was Gordon who somehow had dissuaded her from marrying that loopy boy she met in her first year at university. (That would have been a disaster.) And when, a couple of years later, she and Barry had slid off to marry without telling anyone, he'd somehow managed to persuade her mother that it was not the slap in the face it seemed. (Though Tory, colouring at the memory, would not forget what Gordon said to her and Barry once he had got them alone.)

No, she'd been really, really fond of him. He'd been a brick.

So was she sad? Well, yes, of course she was. But it was not as if someone her own age had died. Or, God forbid, someone her children's age. Gordon must be – must have been – well over seventy. That wasn't bad. And he could not have popped his clogs a better way than dying in his sleep so peacefully that Mrs Deloy didn't even realise when she first peeped round the door. So what would it have been? Heart attack? Embolism? Something along those lines in any case since, when they last met at the hospital, only two nights before, he had seemed somewhat tired but otherwise perfectly well.

Oh, God! The hospital! Megan would be itching to get up there to give their mother the bad news. And no doubt during the drive she would go on and on at Tory about not carrying her phone. 'What if it had been one of the children?' That sort of thing.

But bad news travelled fast enough.

Unlike this bloody bus.

*

'Ready?'

'I suppose so.'

Megan pushed open the door. Unusually, their mother was sitting up against the pillows, looking quite perky. 'Hello, dears. You're very early. And together, too.' She managed to stop herself from adding, 'That's a bit of a surprise!' Still, both the sisters heard the words ringing unspoken round the little white room.

They let their faces do the work for them.

'Darlings, is something wrong?'

Megan perched on one side of the bed and patted Elinor's hand. 'Horrid news, actually. I'm really, really sorry.'

Tory resisted the temptation to butt in, saying, 'So am I,' and went round the other side.

Elinor looked from one of them to the other. 'Gordon? Is it Gordon?'

Megan nodded. 'I'm afraid so.'

'Has something happened? What? A heart attack? A stroke?'

Tory almost admired the way that Megan was shaking her head and somehow managing to make her face look even more mournful.

'No!' said their mother. 'He's not—?'

'Yes,' Tory said, to put an end to it. 'It seems he died in his sleep sometime last night. Mrs Deloy looked in on him this morning, and she phoned Megan.'

Elinor turned to Megan as if Mrs Deloy's choice of phone number had given her elder daughter some sort of imprimatur as next-most-bereaved. 'Oh, darling!'

Megan tried to look brave.

'Worse for you, Mum,' said Tory, almost sharply.

'Much worse,' said Megan.

But Elinor Forsyth managed to look no more than baffled. 'I can't believe it,' she said. 'Dead? Just like that? In his sleep?' She gave herself a little shake. 'And I was saving such good news for him when he came in this morning.'

Tory recalled a story Barry told her once about some ancient aunt of his who, solemnly informed of her own husband's death, said, 'Lord, that is terrible. Mind you, I had a shocking night myself.' Disguising her snort of amusement as a sob, she turned away. When she looked back,

Megan had leaned closer over the bed and taken her mother's hand. 'Good news, you said?'

'Yes.' All at once, Elinor seemed breathless. 'Those scan results came back. Dr Nagpal says there's no more spreading in the lungs or liver. And one of the string of nodules on my chest wall has shrunk.'

'That's excellent news!'

Tory stood waiting, and in the end Elinor did force herself to admit the rest of it. 'Annoyingly, they did find a tiny bit more spread along the spine.'

'Probably very slow though,' Megan comforted her. 'And not much.'

'I don't know, dear. She did go on about the vertebrae. I couldn't follow at all. But she did say it was quite good news on the whole.'

'I'm very pleased.' Megan looked to Tory for support. 'You're pleased too, aren't you, Tory? That's great news.'

It was the bullying that Tory couldn't stand. Small wonder that they tried to come at different times. Megan might choose to ignore the facts, even the fatal prognosis (she'd probably read too many of those stupid 'Mind over Matter' articles while she was waiting for the hairdresser to start on one of her endless 'trims'), but Tory wasn't going to knuckle under. Mum was soon going to die and that was that.

At least this time there was a sideways let-out. 'The thing is, Mum, that there are procedures to be followed and things to be done, and even if your treatment's going well, you probably won't be home for a few days.'

'No, dear. I probably won't. Though I am feeling better.'

But bloody Megan wouldn't stop. 'You look miles better.'

'That's what Nurse Connaught said.'

Tory dragged both of them back. 'So shall we just get on with it – the two of us? I mean, we can bring in the forms and whatnot for you to sign.'

'Forms?'

'You know. Whatever.' Tory spread her hands. 'I'm sure there will be loads of paperwork. That's what they always say – that it's a full-time job, sorting things out after a death.'

'I'm sure that Gordon was always very organised. Even about this sort of thing.'

What could she mean, thought Tory. This sort of thing? A death was death.

At least now Megan was firmly on her sister's side. 'Yes, Mum. I'm sure he was. But Tory's right. There will still be a huge amount to do. Closing up bank accounts and stuff. Arranging the funeral.'

'I do believe he's got a file on all of that stuff.'

Tory was staring. 'A file? Really? What, with the music and readings that he wants?'

'Everything, dear. Gordon felt quite strongly about funerals. He's even put aside the details of some sort of basketwork coffin. He always said he couldn't bear to see the waste of seasoned wood.' She brushed away her daughter's astonishment. 'Don't look so surprised, Tory. By the time you reach our age, pretty well the only things you get invited to are burials and cremations. Gordon will have everything worked out. You mustn't panic. It will all be in the file.'

'What, under "D" for "Death"?'

Megan glared, but Elinor only chuckled. 'I wouldn't be at all surprised. Yes, under "D" for "Death".'

And it was only then that the news hit their mother properly and she began to weep.

*

Elinor had not been joking when she said, 'Under "D" for "Death",' for that's where they found it.

'Blimey,' said Tory. (She'd been admiring the alphabetical order of the cabinet. Airmiles. Appliances. Boiler Instructions. Cars. Credit cards. A whole life neatly filed away.)

Megan made a wry face. 'Can I get past you into that bottom drawer? He probably has a copy of his will in W.'

He did.

As her sister unfolded the sheets of photocopied paper, Tory begged for assurance. 'We don't have to tackle that as well?'

'No, no. I only thought I ought to check that it was still the same solicitor.' Megan dropped the sizeable envelope back in the drawer. 'I'll let them know.'

They took the Death file into their mother's kitchen. 'I'll make some coffee,' Tory said as Megan started dealing sheets of paper onto the table.

'Mum was quite right,' said Megan. 'Here's a brochure of biodegradable coffins and he's ringed the one he wants.'

Tory leaned over. 'It looks rather nice.'

'It's all in here,' said Megan. 'The entire funeral. He wants it at the crematorium. A Bach cantata as people come in, more Bach as he goes out.' She saw her sister's puzzled look. 'Slides back behind the drapes. You know. And then some Mozart as the rest of us leave. No vicar. No religious readings. Only a poem by someone called Laurence Binyon.'

'Is that the "They shall not grow old" guy?'

'This one is called "The Burning of the Leaves".'

Tory pulled up a chair. They sat in silence, sipping coffee without milk and reading the chosen poem. 'Bit gloomy,' Tory ventured when she reached the end.

'Quietly suitable,' said Megan. 'And it'll save us having to think.' She rooted further through the file. 'My God! A list of all the people we're supposed to invite.'

Tory stared at the neatly printed pages of names, postal and email addresses and phone numbers. Through several of the names there was a thick black line. 'I suppose these crossed-out ones are dead. He must have kept it very up to date.' She touched a name with her finger. 'It's only a few weeks since he told me he was going to this one's funeral.'

Megan was counting under her breath. 'Forty or so. That isn't bad.'

'He kept in touch with quite a lot of friends,' said Tory, not grasping that her sister's mind was on the catering. She pushed the file away with a great shudder. 'Oh, it's too horrible. I'd hate to think about my own bloody funeral. I couldn't even bear to write a will.'

Megan pushed her chair far enough back to turn to look at her sister. 'Tory, you surely have a will?'

'No.'

'But you must! I mean, what happens if you die?'

'Somebody else's problem.' Tory made a face. 'It's not as if there's anything to fight about. Anyone who comes is more than welcome to the mortgage and the credit card repayments.'

'But what about the children?'

'Sorry?'

'You know. If you and Barry died at the same time. Surely the two of you have got it written somewhere what'll happen to them.'

'What do you mean, "what'll happen"?'

'Well, where they'd go. Who they would live with? I mean, would they come to us, or go to Barry's sister and brother-in-law? That sort of thing.'

'Have you done that, then?'

'Yes, of course we have! Everyone does!'

'Not everyone, Megan.' And, grinning, Tory tapped the file in front of her. 'We don't all get things nicely organised years in advance, like Gordon.'

There was that smug tone in her voice again. Megan bit back her response. What was the point in saying words like 'irresponsible' to Tory and Barry? It was a high road to nowhere. In any case, it barely mattered any more. Lindy and Lou were certainly old enough to choose their own futures. And Ned, however young, would have the comfort of his sisters who, with that long age gap, had always been deputed tasks like fastening him into his car seat and scouring around for something to put in his lunch box. They'd always ordered him about. 'Ned! Put your shoes on now!', 'Stop picking your nose.'

Ned would survive.

And Tory wasn't going to die, in any case. And certainly not in tandem with Barry. So, irritated as she was by the sheer lack of forethought and parental care her sister had revealed, Megan would not pursue the matter.

It made it easier though, to come out with what she said next. 'I'm leaving all this here for now. I have to pick up Malcolm so we can go and get the other car.'

Tory gave one of her smiles. Megan understood perfectly well that what she meant by it was, 'And of course Malcolm couldn't possibly catch a bus as far as the garage.'

But she didn't care.

*

Gordon Forsyth's solicitor steepled his fingers as he studied Megan across the table. 'Now this,' he said, 'would be a question relating only to your mother's will?'

'That's right,' said Megan. 'I just thought, while I was here…'

'Pick my brains. Why not? And, to be frank, it couldn't be more simple. Your stepfather left everything to your mother. And that was mutual in that, if she'd died first, everything she owned would have gone straight to him.' He paused. 'That is by no means always the case, of course. Especially in what we sometimes call "reconstituted" families. You know – with steps and halves and so forth.' He sucked his steepled fingers momentarily. 'But since Mr Forsyth had no children of his own and, as I gather, was around for almost all of your childhood—'

'Since I was eight.'

'Clearly your mother trusted him to do the same if she went first: that is, leave the great bulk of the estate equally to you and your sister.'

'But that's the problem,' Megan explained, 'because, the way things are, it won't be equal.'

His eyes dropped to the paperwork as if in search of some snag that must have escaped him. Megan tried to hurry things along. 'You see, it's the legacies for the grandchildren. When my mother and Gordon drew up these wills, my sister and I both had two children. But now Victoria has three.'

He was still puzzling, so Megan pressed on. 'That means that, when my mother dies, a part of my half-share will end up paying for my sister's last child.' Megan leaned forward. 'I find it very hard to believe that was what either of them had in mind.'

Was she imagining it? Had his look cooled? Well, he could be as snotty as he liked. He wasn't her solicitor and he wasn't Mum's. She was just asking a quick question while she was there on matters to do with Gordon.

'Does this—?' He cleared his throat and started over again. 'Does this – what shall I call it? – this perceived anomaly – worry your mother, may I ask?'

Megan didn't care for his use of the word 'perceived'. She told him frostily, 'My mother isn't well. And naturally I wouldn't dream of raising anything along these lines until a good few days after my stepfather's funeral.'

But it was Gordon Forsyth's estate that would be paying for the time to give her any advice. So briskly he told her, 'Changes can always be made. Your mother could amend her will to divide everything into two equal shares, from which you and your sister could pay your respective children's legacies. Or she could alter the amounts left to each child to rectify what you see as a problem. But that, of course, would be entirely up to your mother. She has no legal obligation to do that.'

'But there's a moral obligation, surely.'

Ah! End of interview. 'But we don't deal with moral obligations, I'm afraid.' He stood up, partly to encourage her to leave and partly to speechify. 'With one or two exceptions that can't be said to feature in this case, each of us is free to leave our estate to whomsoever we choose – and, these exceptions aside, quite as unfairly as we please.'

Now Megan took the hint and rose.

'My guess,' he warned her, 'is that your stepfather would have given the matter some thought when your sister's third child was born. As far as I can tell from our few dealings with him, Gordon Forsyth wasn't the sort to leave things dangling.'

Megan couldn't brush aside her memory of the funeral list with all its carefully crossed-out names. 'Perhaps not,' she agreed. 'But if my mother feels the way I do?'

'Then her own solicitor will happily arrange things to suit her better.' He lifted Megan's coat from the hook behind the door and held it out for her. 'Thank you for coming.'

Megan moved towards the door. She couldn't say that he'd been warm. But he had told her what she needed to know. 'I'll speak to my mother after the funeral.'

'Yes. See what she thinks.'

Megan's look soured even before she left the room. She hadn't liked his last words any more than she had cared for 'perceived'.

3.

Not all that many people came to the funeral. A lot of them wrote, of course, but only to Elinor. Barry read out the poem, which seemed at first to most of those listening to be about gardening. Then Barry thundered out the line about going to the fire with never a look behind and most of them grasped the point. The coffin slid from sight. The music swelled.

And it was over.

Thank Christ for that, thought Tory. She had been horribly embarrassed by all three of her children. Lindy had done nothing but scowl, still furious at her mother's rare insistence that she fall in with family plans. 'Why do I have to be there? He's not my stepfather.' Lou, on the other hand, had sobbed throughout, practically whimpering at times, all the while sniffing fruitily in total disregard of Tory's frowns, and tissues passed along by clearly disapproving strangers. That these were just the crocodile tears of an hysterical teenager must, Tory knew, have been quite obvious to pretty well everyone present, since Lou had never taken any interest in her step-grandfather until he offered her this opportunity to be a focal point of hopeless grief at his own send-off.

As for Ned, he had kept banging his shoes against the rung of his seat till she could have brained him.

Infuriatingly, both of her sister's daughters had been unarguably perfect throughout the morning. They'd shown up in their dark St Hilda's uniform, making both Lindy and Lou's chosen get-up appear very garish, and Ned's scarlet sweater look far too casual. Megan only made things worse by drawing Tory aside in order to whisper unconvincingly that her girls' soberness of dress stemmed from the fact that both of them had to be back in class by noon. But this just served to highlight the difference between the attitudes of the respective schools – and, face it, Tory thought, the parents too. Amy and Bethany walked down the crematorium aisle with graceful confidence, smiling a little sadly at anyone who smiled at them. They took their seats and sat, occasionally exchanging quiet words, until their father finished ushering in the last of the older people, and took his place at their side.

Throughout the short ceremony Elinor had sat, rock-faced, between her daughters. Was she in pain, both wondered? Or had the hospital dosed her up so strongly to get her through the morning that she felt nothing? As the last music soared, Barry wheeled up the chair that they had used to bring her in, and she was awkwardly helped, first up from the wooden bench, then sideways down onto the square blue cushion. Seemingly effortlessly, Barry had pushed his mother-in-law up the short ramp the usher had provided, and out between the etched glass doors towards the small display of family flowers set in the courtyard at the entrance to the manicured grounds.

Tory and Megan walked out together, and Malcolm, Bethany and Amy followed. Tory did not look back for fear of precipitating Lou into a further grotesque and noisy fit of affected grief. No doubt the next group of mourners were already gathering on the front steps. The attendant would have to use her skills to winkle Lou out of there before their service started. That's what the woman was paid for, after all – ushering people about.

And Tory was sick to death of Lou – and everyone else. It seemed an age since she'd been free to live her own life. This last week she had missed both yoga and her meditation class. Mum had been very needy – understandably, of course – and Megan had been both tireless and exhausting, making appointments with funeral directors and solicitors and arranging the funeral, all the while taking very good care to delegate enough trivial matters to Tory and Barry to try to disguise the fact that she had taken charge. She'd been a sodding whirlwind. And in between she'd even managed to ferry Bethany – or was it Amy? – to some sort of music exams over in Bramley, not to mention fitting in driving to York to deliver a printing consignment that had been finished too late, apparently, to be entrusted to their usual carrier.

And now look at her, opening the door of a taxi that Tory hadn't even noticed was discreetly waiting by the gates. She gave each of her daughters a warm hug as they climbed in. She must have ordered it to get them back to school as soon as possible.

Now she was coming back to do her duty with the funeral guests.

The Perfect Daughter and The Perfect Mother.

Tory could have slapped her.

*

34

Elinor was so glad to be safely back in her hospital bed. She was exhausted.

Disappointed, too. She had so hoped that the short simple funeral would be a time in which she could, at last, think about Gordon. In all the days before, it had seemed quite impossible to keep him – or his sudden death – properly in mind. Her days had been an endless rush of temperature and blood pressure checks, requests for samples of blood and questions about everything from what she thought she'd want to eat in six hours' time to how her bowels were working. Every time Gordon came to mind, he had been driven out. And in between she'd slept. For hours, fitfully, but with relief.

So she'd had high hopes of the funeral service. She had imagined herself thinking of Gordon throughout, remembering his voice, the tiny grunt he gave whenever he sat down in a soft chair, the little fuss he always made about having to push her reading glasses and her pills out of the way to make room for the tea tray in the morning.

And what had happened? She'd spent the whole time having to control herself. That horrid, ill-bred sniffing. What was the matter with the child? It's not as if Lou (or her sister) had ever come to visit them with any show of willingness or pleasure. Even at Christmas they had managed to act as if these hours spent with grandparents were just time stolen from their busy lives, a tiresome imposition.

What was the problem with Tory, that she could not control her children? If Elinor had ever behaved that way, her mother would have raised a hand to her – only in threat inside a place so like a church perhaps. (Nobody slaps their child in front of an altar.) And yet the gesture would have made it plain: stop that right now, or you will be in big, big trouble the moment I get you outside.

But, no. Tory had sat there quite as tense as herself. And Megan on the other side was clearly having to bite her tongue. Sniff, sniff and snivel, snivel. The child had ruined the service for anyone who cared in the slightest about Gordon. And Lou was plenty old enough to know better. What was she? Twelve? Thirteen now, probably.

She had been a disgrace. An utter disgrace. Lord knows what people thought! And it was so unfair because the deceased had only one funeral. The widow only had one chance to spend it grieving properly. No. Elinor was going to find it very hard to forgive Tory and Lou.

But now she was, thank God, safely away from everyone, back in her hospital bed. 'Just for a couple of days,' Dr Nagpal had told her. 'Just to make sure you're stabilised again after the stress. Then you can get back to life.'

She'd offered Dr Nagpal the grateful smile she seemed to be expecting, and yet her stomach turned. Life! Life alone. Gordon gone. Overnight! Just as the children's father had vanished from her life – without a word of warning, only a grave look from that police officer and those quiet words: 'Elinor Brown? Mrs Brown, I'm afraid I have some very bad news. Really bad news, in fact. The very worst.'

It wasn't the very worst at all, of course. That would have been one of the children – Megan or Victoria – crushed under a lorry's wheels, or choked to death on a stupid mouthful of school lunch. But it was bad enough. She could remember very little of the first few days. (Had she been given pills to keep her going? Probably.) She could recall the funeral. She had a memory of her mother insisting she should sleep over. 'You can't be on your own with the girls tonight. You simply can't.' And she'd been so glad that her mother was there when she woke weeping, suddenly aware that John's body – what was left of it after the crash – was six feet underground. For weeks she'd wept and had nightmares. Each time rain fell, she saw it falling on his grave as if it might depress his spirits just as much as it was depressing hers. When the first frosts came, she thought of him shivering down there in the deepest dark. The first time that it snowed, she stood beside his grave and almost apologised.

Nothing would ever feel as raw as that again. There was an atrophy of feeling that came with age. And just as she and Gordon could no longer summon words to mind on order for the crossword ('I know it! It's got more than one p in it. It's coming!'), so she could not weep – except in self-pity.

Poor, poor Elinor. Alone again.

*

Megan arrived in the morning, straight after dropping off the girls. The ward was not yet open to visitors and Nurse Tanner stepped into her path. 'I'm sorry, but—'

'Just dropping off this overnight bag,' Megan said hastily. 'I thought Mum might need time to pack.'

Nurse Tanner stepped back. 'Of course. Your mother's leaving us today. You and your sister must be very relieved.'

'Very,' said Megan. 'Though Mum still seems so shaky on her pins.'

'She'll feel washed out for quite a while,' Nurse Tanner warned. 'Probably tearful, too. This awful shock hasn't helped. But even a body that's been through the wringer can be a whole lot hardier than it looks.' Over Megan's shoulder she caught sight of one of the other nurses scuttling into a side ward as yet another buzzer rang. 'Now I'm afraid—'

'Of course. I know you're busy.' Megan patted the empty holdall. 'I'll just tuck this somewhere out of the way, and I'll be off.'

*

That afternoon, Tory drove in to pick up Elinor. 'Between two and three is best,' she had been told, but it was three before Barry managed to see off his client and bring the car home, so it was nearly four before she reached the ward.

Dr Nagpal was almost at the end of her round. Nurse Tanner watched as Tory skidded to a halt halfway along the corridor and greeted Dr Nagpal as if the two of them were the closest of friends. 'So glad I've caught you!'

'Mrs Forsyth's daughter,' murmured Nurse Tanner.

'Ah, yes.' The doctor rose to the occasion. 'You must be very glad indeed that Elinor is finally going home.'

'I certainly am.' Out of politeness, Tory lowered her voice. 'I've always thought it must be horrid to have to die in hospital.'

'Die?' Dr Nagpal looked startled. 'Did your mother not tell you? The last results were rather cheering. Much slower spread, and as for that line of nodules across—'

'Oh, yes,' Tory interrupted. 'She did say. And I do see that that everyone is trying to take a positive line to keep her in good spirits.'

Was Tory imagining it, or had the doctor's voice turned frostier and more professional? 'No. Not at all. We're actually rather pleased. Your mother's been responding beautifully. We simply thought that it was better for her to stay under our care until her husband's funeral was safely over. Nobody wanted an unnecessary relapse.'

'But might there be one?' Tory persisted as the doctor turned away. She followed Dr Nagpal along the corridor, away from the door behind which Elinor presumably sat waiting. 'Relapse, I mean?' She searched for the proper way to ask the question, then gave up. The woman was a doctor, after all. Why should Tory mince her words? 'What I mean is, I really thought that she was going to die. That's certainly the impression I was given. Everyone seemed so very gloomy and serious about the prognosis, and—'

Dr Nagpal rested a hand on Tory's arm to stop her. 'Oh, yes. Your mother's going to die. That is for certain. But she might have months of good quality life in front of her. Years, even. The human body can be the most resilient thing. People surprise us all the time.'

'But the prognosis is the same?'

'Oh, yes. I'm sorry. Nothing has changed there.'

'Right,' Tory said. 'Well, just so I know.'

She took off, back towards her mother's room. Dr Nagpal walked on, but Nurse Tanner couldn't help but turn to give Tory a backward glance. How long had she and all the other nurses on the ward been dealing with Elinor's two daughters? Five weeks at least.

Fussy and Tardy. That's how she thought of them. The one continually trespassing in the sluice to replace the perfectly clean flower water in Elinor's small glass vase; the other always rushing in so late she clearly felt herself entitled to ignore the tactfully soft buzzer that marked the end of visiting hours. Sometimes in the dark watches of the night Nurse Tanner caught herself wondering which of the regular ward visitors would irritate her most if she were stuck in bed and sick or dying. To date, neither of the sisters had made it to the top of her imagined list, but both of them were always – always – somewhere in the running.

*

Megan found it hard to believe. She counted the amounts up roughly in her head, and then went back and started over, this time with pencil and paper. Working her way back through the stubs of all the cheque books she'd found in the file, she added up how much her stepfather had given Tory and Barry over the last few years.

It was a huge amount. On several of the cheque stubs the casually trailing noughts went almost to the edge of the amount box, and Megan had to make an effort to keep her ever-lengthening column straight.

It came to a small fortune. As far back as the records showed, Gordon had been giving her sister and Barry oodles of ready money. Why had he done that? And, even more intriguingly, what had they done with it? It

38

couldn't all have been dribbled away on sofas and children's allowances and their occasional holidays and cheap wine. They paid no school fees. They'd lived in their scruffy house so long their monthly mortgage payments can't have been extortionate. And Tory and Barry hadn't even managed to keep their second car on the road!

But there they were, the unmistakable stubs. Five from one cheque book alone. Two in the set of stubs preceding that. Only one in the book before that, but back and back it went, this endless bleeding of their stepfather's savings, through the entire seven years for which Gordon Forsyth had kept his records, and no doubt for a while before that.

Quite unbelievable!

And did their mother know?

Megan looked down to see her own hand shaking. She was furious. And yet, apart from telling Malcolm, she could do nothing. Not for a few days, anyhow. Elinor was only just home, and frail in body and mind. Megan couldn't trust herself to go round there and tell her mother and keep calm. And suppose her mother knew already – had indeed colluded in this injustice? Megan would be even more outraged. What was the thinking behind it? Was it assumed that, since Megan and Malcolm had worked hard enough to live in the way they wanted, and keep their affairs in order, Tory and Barry should have things evened up for them like infants in a nursery? 'Yes, he does have a nice big red balloon. I must get you one too.'

The money must have vanished somewhere. How about gambling? No, surely not. Neither of the pair had ever shown the slightest interest in losing money that way. Indeed, Megan had more than once heard Barry speaking scathingly of all the halfwits clogging up the queues at newsagents, choosing their 'special lucky numbers' for the lottery. And as for Tory, she could be really unpleasant about even the most traditional things like the Grand National. 'I certainly hope that you're not betting on that! Do you know how many beautiful creatures have had to be put down because of that stupid horse race?'

Blackmail, maybe?

No, Tory was the sort to tell the truth and shame the devil, whatever the grubby secret. In Megan's experience, her sister had never been embarrassed enough by some of the things in her past. That boyfriend, for example, who gave her herpes. Her terrible degree. The hurtful way that she and Barry sneaked off to marry without a single word to Elinor and Gordon.

You'd think that that offence alone would have made Gordon a good deal more unwilling to dip his hand in his pocket every few months the way he clearly had. He had expressed his sheer disgust clearly enough. He'd actually summoned Barry into the living room, and dressed him down in Tory and Megan's hearing. 'The way you marry is your own affair. But to humiliate Victoria's mother in this way is absolutely unforgivable. What is your new mother-in-law supposed to say when people ask her why she wasn't at her own daughter's wedding? "They didn't even tell me it was happening"? It is contemptible.'

He'd ordered Barry from the house. And then, when Tory hurried after her new husband, he'd turned his face away as if she were no more than some bad smell that he was letting out the door. Megan had never known her stepfather so angry. It had been weeks before Tory dared come to the house when Gordon was about, and several months before their mother managed to persuade him to let the matter lie.

So strange, then, that they had become the favoured pair for handouts.

So strange. And so unfair.

*

Malcolm was almost beside himself with irritation. 'It might as well be a reward for bad behaviour!'

'I can't believe it myself.'

'I mean, how could a man like Gordon possibly have thought those two deserved to get any of his money at all, let alone keep their snouts in the trough over so many years.' He studied the pencilled list she'd shown him one last time and then went back to rooting through the cheque stubs. 'Could it be some mistake? Some way he had of covering expenses of his own by writing something innocent inside the cheque book?'

'A secret lover? Kept in a little pied-a-terre?'

'But then you'd think he'd have the sense to put our names down every other time to make things look less odd.'

'We'll have to ask.'

He brought his head up sharply. 'Ask who? Ask Tory? Or your mother?'

That was a poser. In the end, they asked both. Next time Megan went to visit Elinor she brought up the topic. As she rinsed cups after their quiet tea, she said as if it had just popped into her head, 'Oh, I know what I was supposed to ask you. You know that I took all of Gordon's paperwork to the executors. Well, there was a tiny query about some cheques made out to Tory.'

'What sort of query, dear?'

Megan had thought this one through. 'Perhaps,' she said in what she hoped was a joking tone, 'they just wanted to know whether "Tory" written on the stubs was really Victoria, and not Gordon secretly funding the Conservative Party behind your back.'

Her mother failed to look amused, and all she said was, 'No, no. That money would have been for your sister.'

Megan kept her voice as casual as she could. 'Was it for anything in particular?'

Elinor could not have sounded less concerned. 'Oh, I don't know.' She waved a hand. 'It might have been to help them buy the camper van. No, that was years ago! So I expect it was to help them get started on the business of the painted furniture.' Elinor sighed. 'You know those two as well as I do, Megan, and it's always something.'

'You didn't think that was—?' Megan stopped herself in time. 'You didn't mind?'

'Mind? No, not really. After all, it was Gordon's money. And both of us did really hope that Barry might make something of himself if he fell in the right job.'

Megan had to turn her face away to hide her fury. Fell in the right job! You don't 'fall in' a job. You force yourself into the first one possible, and then you force that job to work, and force yourself to stay in it till something better comes along. That's what you do. You don't just idle about, sponging when necessary off a man you didn't even have the courtesy to invite to your wedding!

That camper van! Ridiculous! Barry had driven all the way to Alnwick to pick it up. Even before he'd got it home, he'd realised that it needed a new clutch and four new tyres. Between them, Barry and Tory had knocked up a passable website, hoping to rent out the vehicle for easy money, then buy a second camper van with the profits. Onwards and upwards. But all the potential clients seemed to want the van during the same few weeks. And even when the dates worked out, the first lot often failed to make it back on time. (The camper van was never quite reliable.) Barry would hurriedly have to track down another vehicle that he could hire to solve the problem, and that would almost always leave him out of pocket.

As for the painted furniture, that plan had maddened Megan from the start. For one thing, the craze for that sort of cheap and cheerful stuff was pretty well over even before Barry came up with the plan. He and Tory had rented a workshop with display space in a nearby town. 'It's unbelievably cheap! A total steal!' But it turned out the place was available only because the business that was hastily abandoning it had realised that the coming improvements to the ring road would put paid to any footfall past the property for a full eighteen months, and possibly longer. If even a well-established shop like China & Chintz had reckoned they no longer stood a chance on Amen Corner and it was worth a move, how could her sister and brother-in-law ever have hoped to make a go of it?

But had the two of them bothered to check with the council to see if traffic plans were pending near the business that they planned to open? No, they had not. So why had Gordon funded these idiotic schemes, and probably several others? He'd been a sensible man himself.

Better ask Tory or Barry.

*

Malcolm asked Barry. It was a couple of days after Tory's most recent trip to see her mother. Elinor had held out through the slow walk around the garden to gauge the ravages of recent neglect. Then she turned back to look at the house and burst into tears. 'I just can't stand it, Tory!'

'It must be awful,' Tory sympathised. 'But it's still early days. And you know you can always come and muck in at our house till you feel better.'

Elinor suppressed a shudder. Luckily, Tory didn't notice. She just pressed on. 'And I know Megan feels the same. You're always welcome there.'

'It's not the loneliness,' wailed Elinor. 'Or even not feeling back on top after the operation. It's so much sillier than that.' Her voice rose shrilly. 'It's what's in the cupboards, Tory! I feel as if I'm being haunted! There are things of Gordon's everywhere, and I don't have the strength of mind to sort them out.' While Tory watched, she blew her nose, then said, a bit more calmly, 'I'd shove the whole lot in the bin, except that some of it is really nice. It's far too good to chuck. But I can't bear the thought of asking Mrs Deloy to take it to the charity shops in town because I might walk down the street and see someone wearing one of Gordon's favourite shirts or jackets, and I couldn't bear that!' She blew her nose again. 'Please, Tory! Take it all away and sort it out. I'm sure that there are things Barry might like. And even Malcolm – maybe a few nice things like the gold cufflinks? I think I'd like the two of them to have first pick from everything – so long as they remember never to wear it anywhere round me.' She wiped her eyes. 'And then the rest of it can go to charity in some place nowhere near here. Megan and Malcolm's firm deliver all over, don't they? Can't one of their vans get rid of all the rest somewhere that's miles away?'

'Of course they can,' soothed Tory. And then, because she knew Megan would fuss if she thought all of Gordon's rather good belongings had just been shovelled out, she added, 'Look, Mum, tomorrow's Saturday so Megan will be driving Amy over to Bramley for her music lesson. Why don't you go along, just for the ride? And while you're out of the house, Barry and I will whisk all of Gordon's stuff away to our house. Malcolm can come round at his convenience to see if there's anything he wants.'

She felt quite saintly, well aware her house was cluttered enough, and reckoning it might be weeks before busy, busy Malcolm showed up to sort his way through everything that was on offer. But the idea of being rid of all the stuff appealed to Elinor so strongly that even before Tory had reached the end of the suggestion, Elinor had agreed.

*

Malcolm, to their surprise, took almost no time at all to make an arrangement to come round to Tory and Barry's house. Together he and Barry rooted through the heaps of clothing on the upstairs landing. Tory had not found time to sort Gordon's belongings into sensible piles, so Malcolm would lift a stylish raincoat only to find a pair of faded Y-fronts clogging up a sleeve.

'Nice shirts,' he said approvingly. 'Pity that Gordon and I had such different neck sizes. But you'll do well.'

'I wouldn't wear them,' Barry said. 'Too smart and crisp for me.'

Malcolm forbore to mention that the Challoner family's laundering skills would soon put paid to any problem there. He sorted through the cufflinks.

'Take the lot,' Barry encouraged him. 'I never use the things myself.'

'But some of these are gold.'

His brother-in-law shrugged. 'So?'

'Well,' Malcolm said. 'They might be worth a bit.'

'I suppose they might.' But Barry said nothing more, so Malcolm took the opportunity that had arisen to broach the topic. 'Talking of money, Barry, do you mind if I ask you a rather odd question?'

'Fire ahead.'

'Did Gordon ever lend you anything? Money, I mean?'

Barry put down the sleeveless pullover he'd been considering and picked up a chunky sweater that had seen better times. 'He was quite good to us, old Gordon, whenever we got stuck. He subbed me quite a lot for all those new windows. Even threw in the cost of a decorator after the joiners explained that unless they were painted promptly we'd just be throwing good money after bad.'

'I can see quite why you're not up to putting in new windows. But as for getting them painted —'

His brother-in-law wasn't listening. 'And he paid up for Lindy's ski trip with school. And one or two other things. The shed, that time I thought I might quite like to be a jobbing gardener. Paid for the strimmer and the mower too, as I recall. No, you couldn't fault him that way. Gordon was really good to me and Tory. I'm sure he would have been as generous with the two of you, if you had asked him.' Dropping the sweater back on the messy pile, he added curiously, 'Did you, ever?'

'No,' Malcolm said. He tried to keep his voice calm. 'No. We never did.'

*

'It is astonishing,' said Megan. She screwed the lid back on the mustard pot and handed it to Malcolm. 'You're saying that he just came out with it? Without even being pressed?'

'Happy as anything to tell me about the handouts he could remember.'

'Tory was just the same! I dared to ask her, "Did you ever think Gordon might have had his doubts about the camper van business or the painted furniture?" And she said, "Oh, I'm sure he thought that we were

44

crazy." Then she went on to tell me perfectly cheerfully about two other things he funded. One was the time she went round nagging everyone to buy that jojoba rubbish, and the other was when they took out that mad franchise to sell those hideously expensive dog toys.'

'We wondered how they'd raked up the money to pay for that franchise. Do you remember?'

Megan moved the last of the dishes onto the draining board and started wiping the kitchen table in angry, swooping circles. 'God, how much of his loot have that pair dribbled away! Gordon must have had a lot more than we ever realised.'

'Certainly more money than sense.'

'And less sense than we thought. Small wonder that there were so many cheque stubs.'

Malcolm took quick advantage of his wife's back being turned to take out the serving plate she'd just jammed in the dishwasher and slide it in again somewhere more sensible. 'I'm just surprised at him. Surely he can't have held out much hope for them getting permanently on their feet – not after the first couple of mad schemes, anyhow. And I can't see why he would think of those two as a worthy charity.' He tipped the last of the cutlery into the basket. 'Maybe he always coughed up just to please your mother.'

'Or to spite me.'

Malcolm looked up. 'Spite you? Why would he want to do that?'

She rinsed her sponge in the sink. 'I don't know. But I wasn't nice to him when he came on the scene. Perhaps he bore a secret grudge and, rather than take it out on me so that I noticed, he found it easier to favour Tory.'

'It wasn't all that secret though, was it? I mean, you and I never realised. But that's presumably because we never thought to ask. Now that we have, it's spilled out easily enough. They certainly didn't try to hide it. And neither did your mum. You said that when you first mentioned the cheque stubs to her, she was as laid back as could be.'

'I got the feeling that she couldn't have cared less.'

'Perhaps that's where your sister gets her easy-come, easy-go ways with other people's money.'

'It certainly has been easy-come for Mum,' said Megan bitterly. 'But I did always think that was sheer luck – Gordon being in such financial clover when she took up with him.'

He grinned. 'You're wondering now if that was maybe part of the attraction?'

Megan scowled. 'I don't know. I don't know anything anymore. I suddenly don't recognise my mother and I have never understood my sister.'

He watched her as she went round one last time, wiping off every last crumb and smear until the kitchen was perfect. 'There's one odd thing,' he said as he hung up the tea towel she had handed him. 'If all four of them always took these loans as casually as everyone pretends to take them now, I'm just surprised we never heard of them before. Don't you suppose that smacks a little of skulduggery?'

Megan recalled with some unease the deep suspicions she'd once held about her husband's dealings with Miss Tallentire over the cow byre. What was that proverb? 'A man never looks behind the door unless he has stood there himself'?

Rather than answer, she pretended that she hadn't heard.

4.

Though it was Amy's turn to take the front seat on the drive to school, she chose the back. 'I have to revise for the test.'

She tried to concentrate. But still she couldn't help hearing the chatter between her mother and sister. First it was all about what Bethany might want to do on her birthday. Then they went on about a tramp who'd stumbled off the kerb. And after that, and seemingly out of nowhere, Bethany asked, 'Will Granny get all Gordon's money now?'

'Yes. Yes, I suppose she will.'

'So she'll be rich.'

'She'll certainly be better off than before. And she's not badly off now.'

Bethany stared out of the window for a while, and then she asked, 'How rich?'

Amy could not resist it. From the back she called out, 'Stinking rich.'

Megan's eyes met her daughter's in the rear view mirror. 'What makes you say that, Amy?'

'I just know.'

'How?'

Would it end up in trouble? Amy could not see how. 'Because Lucinda's dad is Gordon's stockbroker and she was listening one day when he was on the phone. She isn't stupid and she knows a lot about her father's job. She says that, from the things she overheard her father saying, Gordon has to be dripping with money.'

'Had to be,' Bethany corrected her. 'Because he's dead.'

'This isn't a nice conversation at all,' said Megan. 'I'm going to suggest we start all over again.' Her tone turned bright. 'What are your plans for today, Bethany? Will you be practising in the lunch hour? Or is it canteen supervision?'

Bethany did sigh, but she was well enough brought up to give a civil answer. Amy, meanwhile, turned her attention back to revision.

*

Tory had much the same conversation with her own family. Ned started it at one of the few suppers she'd had the energy to force him to eat at the table, rather than simply snatch up and take back to whichever screen he was currently favouring with attention.

'Will Gran inherit all of Gordon's loot? Or will we get some?'

Tory considered. It didn't sound a pleasant question. It was graspingly put. But still she couldn't think of any reason not to answer him. 'I think we'll get some in the end, but not right now.'

Lindy was quick off the mark. 'Do you mean when the solicitors have finished sorting Grandpa's stuff out properly? Or only when Gran's dead as well?'

Tory wished Barry was about so she could start up some totally different conversation with him to head the children off. But he was out, buying a pint for Eddie from the garage as thanks for fixing their car after his official hours, and toning down the bill. So in the end she said reprovingly, 'It isn't nice to think ahead to someone else's death.'

'But Gran is dying, isn't she? You said so. So why shouldn't I ask?'

Remembering the look on Dr Nagpal's face when she had raised this very topic, Tory felt even more uncomfortable. 'It might be quite a while, so there's no point in talking yet about what happens after.'

'You said that it would happen very soon.'

The accusation hung there. Was she supposed to feel she'd let them down, leading them on and now expecting them to wait? 'Well, yes, it might be sooner than we think. But then again the body is a very unpredictable thing. It might be ages.'

'Yes, yes.' Lou rolled her eyes to show impatience with her mother's fence-sitting. 'But after it finally happens, will we be rich?'

'Lou!'

Ned came to Lou's defence. 'Why can't she ask? I want to know as well. Will we be rich? Will I be able to buy a new Star7?'

Lindy pitched in. 'The first thing I'm going to do is go shopping at that new place in The Courtyard. They have the most amazing stuff.'

'I want a new phone too, like Ned.'

'And me! The one I've got is crap.'

Tory stood up. Usually she at least made the effort to ask one of the three of them if they would help her stack the plates, but this time she was glad to turn her back and clatter things onto the draining board.

Were other people's children quite as mercenary and outspoken as this? What had gone wrong? She'd tried to raise them in a way that let them all develop naturally, never imposing rules she didn't think were truly justified. And she'd fetched up with this unpleasant, grasping rabble.

Then Lindy's crap phone rang.

'Please don't answer that,' said Tory. 'Not while we're at the table.'

'I've finished, though! I don't want any more!' Triumphantly, Lindy slid off her chair and rushed away. Taking this as permission, Lou reached in her pocket for her own phone. Ned had already vanished.

Tory turned to the sink. God, just one evening coping on her own was driving her insane! No, half an evening, thank God, for there was Barry, looming through the frosted glass, seemingly fumbling for the key he didn't need because the door wasn't locked. She let him in. 'Good time?'

'Not really,' he confessed. 'He is a bit of a bore. But duty done.'

'Same here,' she said. And then, feeling the urge to spend some time in company she chose instead of that forced on her, Tory burst out, 'Why don't we say sod it to everything, invite a load of people round a week on Friday and have a party?'

Barry had just heard enough from boring Eddie about his family's coming travel plans to be able to tell his wife, 'That weekend's Easter.'

'Then we'll have an Easter party.'

Barry knew when there was a point in arguing, and when there wasn't. So he just shut up.

*

'A party?' Megan was startled. 'Are you serious?'

Tory could not help making a face at her sister. 'What's so wrong with that?'

'But it's so soon!'

'Easter? It's getting on for a whole fortnight away.'

'I didn't mean so soon from now. I meant, so soon after Gordon's funeral.'

Tory laughed. 'I wasn't thinking of inviting Mum. I was just telling you I won't be able to go round to her place that evening or the one before. I was just checking you'd be around so you could pop in on her.'

'Still…' Megan said.

'For heaven's sake!' snapped Tory. 'Don't be so po-faced, Megan. Just because you and Malcolm never socialise!'

And then she went bright red as Megan turned away, for both of them were suddenly remembering Megan's last party – possibly not the very last Megan and Malcolm had held, but certainly the last to which Tory and Barry had been invited. It was a horrid evening, and even Tory was ashamed of what she'd done.

'Come as a personality,' Megan had told her. 'It's not quite a fancy dress party, like the ones you and Barry have. I don't think Malcolm's friends are quite as lively as that. But we thought we could at least ask everyone to come as someone other than themselves, then people can break the ice a bit by trying to guess.'

Tory had started off by thinking of the person Barry should be. They'd run through plenty of politicians and one or two pop stars, but in the end they'd settled for a famously demented telly chef. Barry tracked down the heavy-duty stick-on moustache and the straw yellow wig, and waving his ladle and spaghetti server in the air, he had looked just the ticket. Pretty well everyone at the party would know who Barry was supposed to be.

For herself, she'd had more of a problem. She had dismissed out of hand the idea of dressing up as one of the women on television or in politics whom she admired. Some wouldn't do because they were so very much slimmer; others because she told herself that any friends of Megan's or Malcolm's were most unlikely to know who they were. She obviously wasn't going to turn up in proper fancy dress, as Little Miss Muffet or Marie Antoinette or anyone like that. And then the idea came. She wouldn't tell a soul what she was planning, but she'd gone searching round the charity shops three days in a row. Barry kept asking her, 'What's in that bag?' and, 'What are you planning?' but she wouldn't offer him the smallest clue. As late as the evening of Megan and Malcolm's party, Barry had no idea who she was going to be.

They dressed together in the bedroom. 'Get a move on,' he warned. 'The taxi will be here in a few minutes and you've not even started tarting up.'

'No make-up needed,' she announced. While he tugged on his wig, she climbed into a rather sober skirt. 'Kirsten MacKay!' he guessed, referring to a somewhat prim Scottish private detective from a series they'd been watching on television.

She shook her head. 'No. Try again.'

But he was far too busy with the glue for his moustache. And by the time the two of them climbed into the taxi, he still hadn't made another stab at guessing who she was supposed to be.

'Well?' she demanded.

He turned to look at Tory properly for the first time. Even in the liverish glow of street lamps, it was quite obvious. Her hair was held back on both sides by matching mock tortoiseshell barrettes. Apart from the religiously powdered nose, her face was free from make-up. The blouse she wore had just a frill too many and the pleated skirt, though it had obviously been expensive, was somewhat drab.

'Christ!' he said. He was truly horrified. 'You cannot do this, Tory! We must go home. You'll have to change.'

'Nonsense!' she said. 'It's funny.'

'No, it's not.'

And he was right. Nobody at the party thought it either clever or amusing to ape the hostess. Was it poor Megan's fault that she lacked style, and was too busy working in the firm and monitoring the lives of her young daughters to spend time leafing through fashion magazines and asking for advice on shop floors? Finding herself abandoned by every person she approached – 'I must just nip to the loo.', 'Forgive me! There's something I forgot to say to my friend over there,' – Tory soon realised that she'd gone too far. She took out the barrettes, but at that stage in the party nobody even noticed that her flying hair no longer matched her sister's more restrained style.

In the end, she and Barry crept away without a proper goodbye. Megan, in any case, had managed to avoid her after that first hurt look. No response ever came to Tory's craven note of thanks. (She hadn't dared to risk the phone.) And it was several weeks before the sisters had met again, most probably at Christmas, and almost certainly as a result of a some invitation sent to both families by Elinor and Gordon.

Who'd want reminding of that horrible occasion? So Tory hastily said, 'Actually I don't even know why I call it a party. It'll just be a few of our closest friends coming for supper. Not really a party at all.' And Megan stiffly replied, 'That's perfectly all right. I can look in on Mum that evening. It'll be a pleasure.'

*

It was a hopeful and vain boast, since few of the evenings Megan spent with her bereaved mother offered much pleasure. The visit on the following day found Elinor in a shocking mood. For one thing she was furious with Mrs Deloy, who'd let it be known while wiping smears off the fridge that she thought the clearing out of Gordon's closets had been a sight too quick for common decency. 'You've never been and got it over with already! Well, that was pretty sharp.' (She didn't actually add, 'The man is barely cold,' but Elinor as good as heard her think it.)

And Elinor's next-door neighbour had annoyed her mightily. Two hours before Megan arrived, Elinor had been sorting out a dresser drawer. Hearing the gate creak, she'd moved towards the window and spotted Anne Taylor coming up the garden path. Elinor backed out of sight, ignoring the knocking on the door until it stopped. Once she was fairly sure that she was safe she'd crept downstairs, only to find the woman peering at her through the back kitchen window.

Sighing, Elinor unlatched the door. 'Oh, I am sorry. Was that you knocking? I just thought it might be—' Hard up for any notion how to finish the excuse, Elinor allowed her words to trail away. Anne Taylor wasn't listening anyway. She had come on a mission. 'It's about that garden wall.'

'The wall?' Elinor was astonished. She had assumed her tiresome neighbour had at least come round to say again how very sorry she was that Gordon had died, and how much she regretted not being able to attend his funeral.

'The shared wall.'

'Shared?'

'Yes.' Anne Taylor stepped inside. 'I'm sure you've noticed that it's all of a crumble. I did keep saying as much to Gordon, and he kept promising that he'd look into it. But over this last winter it's got worse and worse, and now I really feel we ought to tackle it.'

Elinor drew herself up. The horrid breathlessness was back today, but she was cross enough to get through her rebuke. 'I am so sorry. I had no idea that, while I was so very ill in hospital, then busy sorting out my husband's funeral, that you were worrying about something so vital.'

Anne Taylor's face reddened. 'Elinor, I do appreciate that—'

But Elinor had already opened the back door, and was standing there waiting. Anne Taylor tried to salvage something of her dignity. 'You'll give it some thought, will you, Elinor? Because I could ask Mr Fletcher down the road to take a look at it. Or we could send out for some estimates, and then I think a sensible thing to do might be—'

Elinor never learned what might have been a sensible thing to do. She had already shut the door behind her neighbour. So by the time that Megan reached her mother's house, she found her in a more peevish mood than any she'd yet seen. Resentment at the visit from Anne Taylor had settled into self-pity. 'Megan, I think I might be going mad. I wake in the morning and I'm convinced that I can hear Gordon carrying the tea tray up the stairs. I actually hear the clinking noise it used to make because he always stacked the cups and saucers. And then I realise it's all in my head, and that another ghastly, endless, miserable, lonely day has begun. Oh, I miss Gordon so much! I weep and weep. You simply can't imagine!'

Oh, can't I? Megan thought, remembering the countless times her mother must have heard Megan's own eight-year-old self, sobbing in the bedroom after that awful car crash – aching and aching to see her beloved father in the doorway, longing to feel his soothing touch, snuggle against his faintly smelling pullover (could he have been a secret smoker?), have him alive again. Her mother must have heard her. The walls and doors in that house had been paper thin. But she had almost never come into the room to comfort her horribly grieving daughter. And when she had, her words had been perfunctory – halfway to irritable. 'Darling, you will get over it, you know. Everyone gets upset when someone dies. But they get better very soon – much sooner than you think. So do stop crying, darling. It just upsets Tory.'

*

Just upsets Tory? Well, we couldn't have that, could we! Nothing was ever allowed to trouble that golden child. So is that how the conversations started? Is that why Megan muttered in her bed for hour after hour to her dead father – simply from stubbornness? She might not be allowed to grieve aloud for fear of bothering her sister. But she could fight back. She could idolise her dad, and keep this perfect vision of him at her side night after night so that when, less than a year later, Elinor took up with Gordon, it truly seemed to Megan as if her own real father were beside her still. No other man could step even into the shadow of his place.

She'd been disgusted by the way her sister fawned upon the newcomer. To this day Megan could recall the way her stomach tightened as she was forced to watch young Tory flirting with him, reading out the feeble riddles from some dog-eared joke book she adored, and greedily peering up to see him smile. Tory spent hours prancing on the rugs in that stupid pink tutu, making up endless little dances and 'shows' till even their mother was embarrassed enough to beg her to stop. 'Let Gordon just get himself another gin and tonic, dear. He'll come back in a while.'

The trouble was, he always did. He came back every time, balancing his fizzing tumbler on the sofa arm and calling out, 'Right, then, Victoria! On with the show!' even if in the meantime Tory had got bored and wandered off. What was the matter with the man? He couldn't have believed he'd only keep himself in Elinor's good books by showing superhuman patience because the woman he was trying to impress had hardly any tolerance for watching Tory showing off. A few ungainly pirouettes, one or two drooping attitudes, and Elinor was on her feet. 'Oh, God! Back in a tick. It's just I think I might have forgotten to…'

She never came back into the living room as promised, in the way that Gordon did. Ten minutes later, Megan – similarly determined not to stay and watch her sister's caperings – might come across her mother reading the newspaper at the kitchen table, or upstairs sorting laundry. But Elinor had always had the gift of never doing anything she didn't choose. Looking back, Megan realised all too clearly that her mother hadn't wanted to remain one of those pitiable widows, so she simply hadn't. Nor had she wanted Gordon to be thought of as a second husband, so she'd fixed that as well. The children's father had been airbrushed out. Megan and Tory's surnames had been changed to Forsyth 'so we're more like a proper family', and Megan could recall her own astonishment at hearing someone's elder sister say at school, 'No, I'm not Cunningham. I kept my real dad's name, so I'm still a Foster.'

Megan had never realised that there was a choice.

Gordon Forsyth had indulged her mother and her sister's every wish. No doubt if Megan had given him the chance, he would have spoiled her as well with something over and above the patient gentleness he showed through all her sulks and moods. He'd been an easy-going man. Tory, in her more socialist phase, had pointed out that being easy-going wasn't difficult if you had pots of money. But even while Megan was so busy hating him for being in their house, and quite sincerely wished him gone, she'd recognised he was a generous man.

And clearly all too generous with Tory's family. All those damn cheque stubs! But even as she sat across from her mother, nodding her head in feigned sympathy while Elinor ran through her litany of complaints about the sheer insensitivity of those around her, Megan knew full well this was not the day on which to raise the topic of the will. Any suggestion now that, with Gordon gone, there was an opportunity to restore parity between the sisters would be interpreted by Elinor in this mood as a brute wish to see her, too, conveniently dead and buried, and the estate dispersed.

Better to soothe. 'You mustn't worry about Mrs Taylor. She's probably hard up for cash and worrying that, if the wall collapses, the bill will be a good deal more than she can afford.'

'Still, dear. To say that to a widow!'

'I suppose she thinks that, since she's a widow herself...'

'Stan Taylor's hardly fresh underground!'

'Mu-um!'

'You know exactly what I mean. That Anne Taylor has had plenty of time to get accustomed to dealing with things herself. The fact that she is on her own as well doesn't give her the right to come and persecute me.'

'It's not quite persecution.'

'I don't know what else you'd call berating a grieving woman about a crumbling wall.'

Oh, it was hopeless. Once Elinor got a notion in her head, no one could shift it. Except for Gordon. He'd been very good at wheedling Elinor round to different views. If only Megan had been able to deal with him.

But he was dead. And it was he who had created the problem in the first place. All very well, thought Megan, for people who had shedloads of money to be so slack about it. There still remained the issue of what was fair.

She would come back to it another day.

*

Elinor shut the door behind her daughter with the greatest relief. She'd managed to get through the evening without Megan daring to bring up whatever grudge was on her mind. Elinor knew that closed, pinched look on Megan's face for what it was – the grown-up version of her ghastly, penetrative childhood sulks.

And they'd been cosmic. 'Why did it have to be my daddy who got killed?', 'Why do I have to live with Gordon just because you like him? Everyone else has their real father!'

Such a persistent child. On and on, reeking of 'poor, poor me' till Elinor could tear out her own hair. She'd even had that frightful dream of creeping into Megan's room to strangle her. (My God, her heart was thumping when she woke. For several moments she had feared she'd have a heart attack.)

The sulks in teenage almost came as a relief. One can ignore a sullen silence and a thick black scowl far easier than a tearful question. It had been so much easier to love silly, empty-headed Victoria. At least she laughed and smiled and danced about, and when she spoke of her dead father it was simply out of cheerful curiosity, or to serve her own purposes. 'Tariq's dad spanks him. Did my dad spank us?', or, 'Did my first dad hate mushrooms as much as I do? I bet he did! It's probably something I inherited. I bet no one tried to make him eat them.'

And all that bloody watching Megan did. Watching to see if Tory ever got a bigger slice of cake, or a more expensive present. Checking to see that Tory's bedtime stayed the same as hers had been at the same age. Insisting that Tory couldn't walk alone across the park until she was eleven. 'I had to wait that long!' Over and over, Elinor had to speak to her about her attitude. 'Such an unhappy way to go about life, Megan. Almost mean-spirited. Not everything is fair, and by and large you'll find as you get older that it doesn't matter.'

Oh, but it did to Megan, who was hair-triggered to spot injustice everywhere. 'My work was just as neat as Tod's, but he got better marks.' 'It's so unfair! All of the holidays this term are on a Monday, so the other class get to go swimming more.'

'Stop it!' Gordon had ordered her on one occasion. 'Just stop it, Megan! That sort of blighted thinking will corrode your soul.'

They'd been astonished that she didn't turn on him. They both stood waiting for the scream of rage, the cries of, 'You can't talk to me like that! You're not my dad!' But then they saw the little plastic buds she'd just that moment jammed deep in her ears, and her short fingers stabbing at the silver square clipped to her jerkin. Reprieve! The music throbbing in her ears had been too loud for her to hear his scathing words.

But he still spoke of her, late in the night. 'Elinor, you must do something. This ghastly habit must be some miserable leftover from losing her father in such an awful way. Surely someone should try to deal with it. Perhaps a therapist...?'

It was the nearest Elinor and Gordon had ever come to quarrelling, and Elinor's annoyance had fuelled her fluency. A therapist, indeed! Why, Elinor had had to watch her father going off to dangerous places – often for months on end. He'd been attached to barracks, though he himself was in 'Security' and not the army. Still, Elinor had stood in assemblies in the local primary school to sing *The Day They All March Home*, and even at that age she'd known that her own father was just as much at risk as all the other children's soldier dads. She'd had that worry hanging over her for years and years. And she'd been fine. So had the twins in her class who lost their father in a helicopter accident. They hadn't needed therapy. And if they'd had it, it would probably have simply caused the loss to register more strongly. There had been something in the paper only days before. She'd dig it out so Gordon could read it. The journalist had said research now showed that dwelling on a bad experience was prone to fortify the neural pathways – in short, just make things worse. And wasn't it a well-known fact that people out of concentration camps who'd put the whole business behind them and never spoke of it again had done far better in life than those who'd reckoned that they'd needed 'therapy'?

Gordon had got the message. He hadn't bothered to look up the article, but he had never talked of therapy again. All he said was, 'Well, she's your daughter, Elinor, and you must do what you think best. But you'll admit the girl's obsessed with fairness, and I'm afraid I won't be tyrannised by someone her age.'

No, nor any other. For Elinor herself was shocked to learn the full amounts he'd handed over to that feckless pair. Can all that spoiling of Tory have been to prove a simple point to Megan? If so, the whole performance had been a singular waste of time. It seemed that Megan and Malcolm had never known.

But they did now.

*

Barry swung by the crematorium in a great hurry. He'd promised Tory she could have the car well before five, and it was half past four already. Christ, couldn't clients witter on! And in this case Barry's determined patience had served no purpose, since Mr Harris had decided in the end that he could easily forgo the added insurance.

Of course the job of picking up Gordon's ashes could have waited. What was the hurry? But as Tory pointed out, he would be passing by the place and she had promised Elinor she'd do the business after that letter came.

Where was the letter? Had he lost the bloody thing? No. Here it was beside him on the passenger seat. The sandwich that he'd bought at lunch time had soaked into it a bit. There was a grease stain on the release form that was attached to it. Barry reached out to pick the papers up as he slowed down between the bushes and the monuments along the winding drive.

That's when it caught his eye – the dotted line without a signature on the 'permission to accept' form. Was he supposed to drive all the way back across town just to get Elinor's signature? Oh, what a massive waste of time!

And who the hell was going to check? Scrabbling inside the over-stuffed glove compartment, Barry unearthed a pen and tried to picture Elinor's signature. It was, as he recalled, a little childish-looking, as if she had been taught to write with an italic pen, but after that her handwriting had never burgeoned into anything more characterful. Easy enough, and Tory wouldn't mind. Rather than having the bother of driving back to Elinor, she would have done the same herself.

*

'I would have done the same myself.'

'I knew you would.'

'Well, job done anyway.' Tory reached for the box that held the urn. 'It's a lot heavier than you'd think.'

'I don't think that they're ashes as we think of them.'

'No time to look now.'

'Not sure I fancy the idea in any case.'

She grinned. 'I must be off.'

'Where are you going, anyway? You never said.'

'It's a knitwear idea. Stephanie read about it in some fancy magazine and thinks it might be a good way for us to make our fortunes.'

He laughed. 'Let's hope it goes better than that daft jojoba business.'

She hated it when he pretended his own ventures were more practical. Or more successful. He was the one who put their money into the expensive things – the hired van business and the painted furniture shop – and left them with the debts they could pay off only when Gordon came up trumps. At least her little schemes were cheap as chips. Never mind. Any evening spent with Stephanie was a good laugh. They'd have a drink or two. (Stephanie always paid.) They'd chat a little about sex – or lack of it. Sometimes the whole idea that she'd been summoned to discuss never came up. Stephanie would kiss her goodbye, then gasp, 'Fuck's sake! I clean forgot to tell you my brilliant plan. Well, never mind. When are you free tomorrow? I'll give you a buzz. We'll talk about it then.'

Sometimes she did. Sometimes she didn't. Tory didn't usually care. Now, glancing at her watch, she shoved the box that held Gordon's ashes right to the back of the coat cupboard, out of the children's sight, snatched the car keys from Barry and rushed from the house.

*

Malcolm was filing away the latest updates of their personal investments when Megan came back from visiting her mother.

'How was she?'

'In a foul mood.'

'Because you asked her about the will?'

'I never dared go anywhere near that. It was because Mrs Deloy had ticked her off for getting rid of Gordon's stuff so fast, and then that ghastly neighbour had come round to moan about the wall.'

'The woman's right, though. That wall is in a dreadful state. I never understood why Gordon refused to get it sorted.'

'Perhaps Anne Taylor annoyed him, going on about it all the time.'

'Still, what's a bit of pointing work, compared to having to rebuild the whole damn thing?'

'Maybe when you're so "stinking rich" you just don't care.'

They both fell silent, thinking of the conversation in the car that Megan had relayed. Malcolm had been astonished. 'Blimey! Lucinda's dad said that about Gordon? I always knew your stepfather was well heeled…'

'That's what we all thought, isn't it? Like he admitted once, "Pleasantly comfortable".'

'But when a stockbrokers like Hendrik Bland & Co you're "dripping with it"...' Now, slamming the file drawer shut, he ushered his wife out of the downstairs office into their spacious hall. On the way up the stairs, she said, 'I am beginning to think—'

'Yes?'

But Megan waited till the two of them were safely in the bedroom, with the door shut. 'I am beginning to wonder if Gordon took a good deal more interest in his money than he let on. I mean, not in the getting of it. Or even keeping it. But in the way that he sloshed it about.'

'Or didn't.'

'Quite. A bit of a power trip, maybe? Who ended up in favour. Who did not.'

'But if we ended up in the same category as Mrs Taylor and her crumbling wall, why didn't he let us know? Where was the fun in it for Gordon if it was all a secret?'

She pulled the coverlet aside to reach for her nightdress. 'Possibly it never occurred to him that Tory and Barry would take his handouts so entirely for granted that they'd never mention them.'

Malcolm slumped on the bed. 'I don't see what he had against you anyhow? You say that you were rude to him when he first came—'

'Not just rude. Really mean.'

'But you'd just lost your dad! And I must say I never thought of Gordon as petty-minded in that way.'

'Don't forget that he had no children of his own. Maybe he didn't make allowances for people being only eight, and dead upset.' She scowled. 'Though he put up with all that fussing Tory could produce. He never seemed to mind that.'

'Mystery. It's a complete and total mystery!'

'The thing is,' Megan said, 'if Gordon was anywhere near as rich as Lucinda's father seems to think he was, then this inequity in the will becomes even more significant.'

'I shouldn't worry about that. Your mother will see sense.'

'Yes. If she ever gets into a calm enough state for me to tackle her about it.'

'Plenty of time,' said Malcolm soothingly. Though both of them, of course, knew that, with one thing and another, time was the last thing that either they, or Elinor, now had.

5.

The results of Elinor's most recent set of blood tests came back a few days later.

'What does it mean?' she wailed. 'All those great technical words. I can't make head or tail of any of it. Why do they want me back? What are they planning?'

'You don't have to go back to stay,' soothed Tory. 'Or, if you do, it will be only overnight. They just want to do one or two more little tests.'

'But why? I thought that I was getting better!'

'These things are complicated,' Tory said, and looked to Megan for help. Usually when Elinor acted like a panicked child, Megan could show more patience. This time, however, her sister seemed distracted. 'I'll make us all some tea,' was all she said, and vanished into the kitchen.

Tory was irritated. Megan couldn't have it both ways. She knew how Tory felt about the business of pretending things were fine – or at least getting no worse. If she expected Tory to sit there spinning lies to bolster up their mother's hopes while she escaped to tinker with the tea cups, she'd got things very wrong. Abandoning Elinor to yet another worried reading of the consultant's letter, Tory followed her sister into the kitchen and shut the door behind her. 'Well, what now?'

Megan swung round, already on the defensive. 'What do you mean?'

'You know,' hissed Tory. 'You are the one who's always telling her that things are tickety-boo and getting better.'

'I've never told her that!'

'You've come as close as damn it. Thanks to you, that's certainly what she thinks. Well, I'm not lying to her. That's your job. So you go back in there and keep it up, as usual. I'll make the tea.'

She tugged the tray towards her, rattling the cups. Megan pulled back. Then Tory suddenly let go. The tray shot back, sending the tea cups flying. Two of them smashed on the floor. The third lay on its side, so badly cracked it would be useless.

'Well done,' said Megan. 'They were her favourite cups.'

'Oh, stuff it!' Tory snapped back.

Now Elinor was calling from the living room, 'Is something broken, dears?' They both ignored the voice as Megan switched into her elder sister mode. 'What has got into you? What is your problem?' and Tory snarled, 'I'm waiting for you to go back in there and tell her that her cups are broken and it really matters because she's going to live for ever!'

Both of them stared at one another. Then Megan said, 'Is that what you think I've been doing?'

'All this while? Yes!' Tory bent down to pick up bits of china. 'And I can tell you that it isn't helping.'

Megan called over her shoulder, 'Not a problem, Mum! Nothing important! Back in a jiffy.' Then she said to Tory, 'I am really, really sorry.'

Tory looked up. 'What?'

'I'm really sorry,' Megan said again. 'I hadn't realised.'

'Honestly?' Tory was astonished. 'You didn't know that that was what you were doing? You didn't realise that every time she slid down one more step, you found some way to tell her that it wasn't happening, or didn't matter?'

'No. I think I just sort of—' Megan's voice was barely audible. 'It's very hard – I mean—'

Tory was staring at her. 'Are you apologising?'

Megan went beet red. 'I suppose I am.'

'Blimey!' And Tory laughed. Patting her sister's hand, she leaned across and lay a smack of a kiss on her pale cheek. 'Now there's a first!'

They both rose. Tory reached behind to push the door ajar between the kitchen and the living room. 'It's my fault, Mum!' she called. 'I turned round without looking and bumped into Megan who was carrying the tray. The cups got broken.'

'Oh, well.' Elinor's voice drifted back sounding not so much philosophical as somewhat baffled. 'It doesn't matter, dears. I don't suppose in any case that I'd have been using them very much longer.'

*

'Your sister actually said that she was sorry?'

'She did.'

'That's not like Megan.'

'Not at all.'

Barry pushed Archie's wet nose away from the cheesy fingerprints along the table edge so he could wipe them off. 'So what do you suppose she's playing at?'

'Nothing. My guess is that she's just been really, really stupid. It's not as if she and Malcolm think much about things, is it? The pair of them just soldier on the way that ghastly newspaper of theirs tells them they should, making their sensible investments and sending their girls to a school that'll give them enough of a dribble of culture to know how to behave in theatres and concert halls. Neither of them ever seems to actually question anything. So I suppose it was just easier for Megan to think that things were going to drift on in the way they have. And that's what she's been doing.'

'So what's got into her now? It's not as if Elinor looks any worse, or has got noticeably feebler. The only thing that's happened is that she's been called back for more tests, and that's happened often enough over the last few years. So why would Megan suddenly find it in her interest to face the truth about how long your mother has to live?'

'Don't ask me.' Tory said. 'All I know is, she's totally changed tack.'

*

Megan could tell from the faint noises coming from behind the door that Malcolm was still working in the small home office, but she walked quietly past and went upstairs. She wanted time to think. Dutifully she poked her head around Bethany's door. 'Everything all right, Beth? Need any help with your homework?'

Bethany palmed the earphone that had been distracting her. 'No, I'm all right. I'll be down soon.'

But Megan hadn't failed to pick up on the furtive gesture. 'Come on, Bethany. You know the rules. Hand it over.'

'I wasn't really listening.'

'Then you won't miss it, will you?' To drive her point home, Megan came across to look at Bethany's work. 'What is it, anyhow?'

'French sentences.'

Megan picked up her daughter's homework notebook and flicked through expertly. 'Exercise sixteen, numbers one to ten?'

Sullenly, Bethany nodded.

'I'll swap you when you've finished,' Megan said. 'I get to see what you've done, and you get this back.'

'I told you,' Bethany said. 'I wasn't even really listening, so I don't care.'

*

Amy was at a rehearsal and wasn't going to be dropped off till after supper. Megan peeled off her clothes and stepped into the shower. Once she was sure her tears would be disguised, she let them fall. What could have happened that she suddenly saw things in such a different light? For Tory had been right. Now Megan knew she had been hiding from herself the fact that they could not go on for ever with their mother in and out of hospital, and nurses popping by the house. It would all end the way it had with Gordon – in a long box.

Another funeral.

And very soon.

So she must make the effort to decide exactly what she wanted before she spoke to Malcolm. Should she bring up with Elinor the fact that things had panned out so unfairly in the past? Remind her mother that she had the opportunity to put things right? It was her money now, so Elinor could make whatever alterations she chose to her own will. This was her mother's chance to make amends for at least some of those cheque stubs! All of that casual 'borrowing' and never paying back! The legacies that wouldn't even out!

Or should Megan bite the bullet and say nothing? Simply accept the fact that feckless Tory, as before – as always – would cream off far, far more than she deserved?

*

Malcolm knew from the moment she came down the stairs. 'Soap in my eyes,' she claimed. But Megan wasn't the sort to let her shampoo trickle anywhere. She had been crying, so he took the conversation carefully.

'Megan, I take your point entirely about the money for the grandchildren. Even though having an extra legacy on their side will eat into what is left for you and Tory to share, I can see how one could just let that go.' He tipped an inch more of the comforting wine into her glass. 'It's all the rest of it. All very well for your mother to tell herself it doesn't matter because we're not as broke as Barry and your sister—'

'Oh, come on, Malcolm. We're not broke at all.'

'Maybe we're not. But there are going to be some hellish big expenses on the way. Seeing the girls through all those university years will cost a packet. And they won't get onto the housing ladder without a deal of help.' He watched her looking to the future with apprehension and added hastily, 'Now I'm not claiming we can't manage it. I'm not saying that at all. All that I'm thinking is that, even though most of Elinor's energy is taken up with something more important, she'll still be grateful for the nudge she needs to put things right before it's all too late.'

His wife scowled. 'I doubt that.'

'Why do you say that?' He tried to harness some of her obvious resentment to tweak the argument. 'She is your mother, after all.'

'It's never bothered her before,' said Megan sourly. 'None of those cheque stubs came as a surprise. In fact, she seemed quite startled that they came as news to me.'

'She can still put things right.' He pressed his case. 'And, Megan, this is cancer that we're dealing with. It is a sneaky illness. If she has patches on her lungs and spine, they'll start to travel.'

'Travel?'

'You know. Up to the brain, and such. And after that it's going to be too late. Your mother won't be in a state to talk to any solicitor about getting the will straight.'

Getting the will straight. That was how he put it. And though she had decided under the stinging needles of the shower that she was done with the whole business – let it go! – Megan had to admit that that's how she still saw it too. It was outrageous that the two of them, Megan and Malcolm, had worked the hours they had, and been so sensible, only to find that all along they had been subsidising Tory and Barry in their easy-going sloth. Those hefty cheques over the years had bled from Gordon's assets. Elinor ought to put it right.

And Megan had seen enough to know exactly what Malcolm meant about the way that cancer could travel to the brain. What was that woman's name – that frail dark creature in the corner of her mother's ward. Such a sweet, gentle soul. Then, practically overnight – oh, horrible! – all of that spitting and cursing, and words all jumbled. All of that struggling to get over the safety rail and out of bed. All of that keening and screaming.

No, he was right. She'd have to grit her teeth and go for it. After all, Malcolm couldn't. And if she left it too late, it would forever lie between them that she hadn't tried.

She offered one small moment of resistance. 'She isn't going to like it. She'll think that I am being ghoulish and grasping. She may even say so to my face.'

He shrugged. His look said plainly, 'What have you got to lose? The woman's dying anyway. She can't be pissed off with you very long.'

She took another swig of wine and giggled. 'Maybe she'll even write me out of the will entirely.'

'I'd say it's worth the gamble.' Malcolm picked up the bottle. There was only a little left, and they had a rule never to open a second. Normally, Megan gave him that little wave that meant, 'No, you can have it.' Tonight, she pushed her own glass forward. 'Thanks.'

He poured the last of the nice Merlot in her glass, aware that the tiny part of him he didn't like was hoping desperately that she would earn it when she finally plucked up the nerve to go to see her mother.

*

Elinor prowled from room to room, unable to settle. She switched on the radio, but a few clumsily spoken lines from *Poetry Please!* sent her straight back to turn it off again. Could they not vet their readers properly? Did no one learn how to speak verse in school? Why did the whole world seem to think that sounding serious and stressing every single word gave added meaning?

Stop it! she told herself. It comes to everybody. Everybody dies.

'Spot welding,' they had called it in the hospital. Spot welding! There the consultant had stood, in front of the lit screen. He'd pointed out this shadow and that blurry patch. He'd rambled on for a while about how they could try this, and have a go at that, experiment with the other. But in the end he'd simply spat it out: 'Spot welding. That's what we're doing now. So, Elinor, it's time for you to tell us what you want.'

What did he mean? Was he expecting her to give him a brave smile and say, 'I won't waste more of your time. Just bung enough painkillers my way to keep me going till the whole thing's over'? Perhaps she was supposed to volunteer for some untested drug? Or crawl away and try to be no more trouble? How about suicide? Was that what he was suggesting? Small wonder they were always telling you to take a friend to consultations – even to record them. The moment you came out, the whole thing turned into a fug. She hadn't got the faintest idea what he was saying or even recommending. It was her own damn fault. She shouldn't have kept the sudden phone call secret. If she'd told either of her daughters, they would have dropped whatever they were doing to come along with her. Then she'd have known what it was all about.

Whose turn was it to pop in on her tonight, in any case?

Friday. So that meant Tory, and thank God for that. Tory at least could lift her spirits – make a joke or two. She wouldn't act like Megan, nagging and scolding to try to unearth the last small detail of the appointment. 'But what did he actually say?', 'He must have suggested something.' No, Tory would allow for Elinor's confusion, as if her not understanding what was going on and what her options were, were par for the course, and probably made almost no difference.

And probably they didn't any more. For Elinor was, as that horribly outspoken vet once said about poor Marmalade, 'on the high road to Nowhere'. But at least Marmalade had not been forced to contemplate the idea of her body rotting underground, or burned to ashes.

Ashes! For heaven's sake! In all the rush of hospital appointments, she'd never thought to ask the girls what they had done with Gordon's remains. She did remember getting a letter from the crematorium. (It was quite sensitive. She'd been impressed.) But had she thought to ask either Megan or Tory to fetch them? Her brain was a blank. She must ask Tory when she finally showed up. (She wouldn't take the risk of asking Megan for fear she'd get in one of her snits. 'Not me, no. I suppose it must have been Tory you asked to do that favour for you.') And what should she do with the ashes, anyway, once she had tracked them down? Presumably in Gordon's file there would have been instructions about that, as about everything else. He certainly had been a man to sort things out. Everything was thought through precisely – right to the bitter end.

The bitter end! What an expression. On with the radio! Was there no distraction anywhere?

It was still *Poetry Please!* – some Easter special, it appeared, to mark Good Friday. Elinor tried to listen. But that galumphing, maudlin northern voice was just too much for her. And by the time that she was rescued by the tapping on the door, she was back in the frame of mind in which she'd left that afternoon's appointment. Scared and resentful. Almost overwhelmed.

*

Megan could tell from the look on her mother's face that she was startled. 'You were expecting Tory, weren't you? Oh, I am sorry.'

Elinor stifled her irritation at the stupid, self-denigrating apology. What was the matter with the girl? If anyone should be feeling a lack of confidence tonight, then it was Elinor. She had a good deal more to worry about than some pathetic little social rivalry between two sisters. 'No. I'm delighted to see you. Come in. Come in.'

Megan followed her into the kitchen and automatically switched on the kettle. Her mother, meantime, opened an upper cabinet to reach for a crystal schooner. 'Sherry, dear?'

'Sherry?' Megan was somewhat shocked. 'Is that really what you're drinking?'

Elinor's face set. 'I don't believe I need to worry about my health.'

'Oh, dear.'

Even to Megan, her tone sounded far more tired than it should. It was a bad start. Elinor was instantly on the defensive. 'Oh, don't you worry, Megan. I'm doing my level best not to become a burden to either of you girls.'

'You know that isn't what I meant at all.'

'What did you mean, then?'

In desperation Megan spread her hands. 'Just that it's all perfectly horrible. You being so ill, and losing Gordon just when you needed him most. And not even being able to go through all these visits to the hospital with any confidence that there's a proper future. It must be ghastly for you. I can't bear to think of it. I don't know how you manage, really I don't. I'm sure I would be halfway to insane.' She took the empty sherry glass her mother was distractedly offering her. 'That's all I meant.'

Elinor was appeased. 'I'm sorry, dear. I didn't mean to snap.'

'That's all right,' Megan said. 'I understand. And I don't mind at all.'

Both of them went through to the sitting room in a far better frame of mind. Elinor asked about the girls, and Megan told her about Amy's play and Bethany's move up to the top set for French. After a while, she felt

69

enough at ease to take the untouched sherry glass back to the kitchen and make herself the cup of tea she'd wanted in the first place.

'More sherry, Mum?'

'I won't, dear.' Elinor changed her mind. 'Actually, I will.'

The thought came instantly to Megan that sherry might be just the thing, so she was generous, filling Elinor's glass to the brim. She kept the conversation on light matters till her mother seemed a good deal more relaxed. Then, drawing breath for courage, she began. 'While we're alone together, can I ask you something personal?'

'Personal?'

'It's about Gordon's will.'

'Oh, that! Tory was asking about that only yesterday. In fact, she phoned up and they told her that it's almost confirmed.'

'Confirmed?'

'You know. That probate business. Well, it's nearly done.'

'Did Tory tell you why she wanted to know?'

Her mother chuckled. 'Well, we all know Tory! She said that she'd been phoning them on my account, but I expect that she was hoping there was something in the offing for her and Barry.'

'And is there? I assumed the whole lot comes to you.'

'It does.'

Megan felt stuck. It was like being in a bog, knowing that any way you stepped you might sink into trouble. But she had spent the whole day fretting, casting around for a good way to bring the subject up. And she'd decided that there wasn't one. The only thing to do, as Malcolm said, was take a chance and risk the consequence.

'I'm glad you get the lot,' said Megan, 'because it did seem that otherwise things might work out in such an unfair way. I'm so relieved you'll have a chance to put things right.'

'Put things right?'

'You know. Rejig them to make up for the fact that Tory and Barry have taken so much money out of the estate over the years.'

Her mother stared at her. 'But that was Gordon's money, dear. Nothing to do with me. I don't think I can fiddle with my own will. I don't think it would be at all right for me to give less to one of my daughters than the other.'

Megan burst out, 'But you've already done that, you and Gordon! You've given that pair huge amounts! Over and over. And Malcolm and I have had nothing.'

The selfishness of other people! Here was Elinor – dying! Dying so soon! And here was Megan, still harping on about her usual obsession – everything being fair.

Elinor's tone was icy. 'I told you, Megan, that was all Gordon's doing. It was no business of mine.' Before her daughter could begin to argue, she was levering herself unsteadily out of her armchair. 'Now, darling, I'm afraid I'm getting the most frightful headache. The doctor told me I should rest as much as possible. So if you don't mind leaving…'

And that appeared to be that.

*

Barry cruised through the Easter party, tossing the long brown hair of his Jesus wig, and spreading his palms to show the lipsticked stigmata. 'No, really. No need to thank me. I was pleased to be of help to humanity.'

Some the guests took a moment to catch on, and one or two looked rather uncomfortable, but he kept at it, passing a mate dressed as the Easter Bunny who was chatting up a friend of Tory's kitted out as an egg with long legs in spangled tights. 'Shouldn't you be at work today?' he asked the Easter Bunny, then, without waiting for an answer, he moved on towards the table with the food.

His wife's friend Stephanie was toying with a stick of celery. Small wonder that she stayed rail thin. She wore a stylish silver frock and a tall golden hat.

'So what are you?'

'Can't you tell? I'm a candle.'

'Oh, so you are.'

'Why are you wearing that nightie?' she asked him in return.

'It's not a nightie. It's a gown.' He spread his crimson-stained hands. 'I'm Jesus Christ, raised from the dead.'

His brilliant get-up was dismissed indifferently. 'I never really learned those Bible stories.' He was about to respond, 'This was the Big One,' and then decided not to bother. This was the woman, after all, who'd tried to persuade his wife to come in on her project to sell cashmere woollies blessed by professional healers, claiming, 'They'll have protective powers. They'll be infused with special holistic energy.'

If you could find a dafter idea on the planet, he'd be astonished.

Another old school friend of Tory's came up, waving a frond of palms. 'You haven't seen my donkey, have you?'

'Last time I spotted him, he'd given up on you and was halfway back to Jerusalem.'

'Oh, well. Pass me those peanuts.' Once the frond man had thrown a handful in his mouth, he nodded at the bottles ranged along the back of the table. 'Any chance of a refill?'

Barry played host with generous aplomb. He'd always enjoyed parties. 'Allow me to introduce you to Candle,' he said before he left. 'But don't forget that fronds can easily catch fire.'

On the top stair, he came across his wife, sitting beside a forlorn-looking girl draped in a weird fleecy top. 'Tory! And a sweet baby lambkin! Do you need topping up?'

Both of them smiled at him gratefully as he refilled their glasses. Tory said, 'Denise here is telling me about her horrid boss. He does sound a real shit.'

Barry spread his stained hands. 'Oh, dear. Because on this day in particular we try to offer forgiveness even to the worst sinners.'

Denise giggled. Tory stretched out her foot to push him skilfully away, and he retreated down the stairs. Was that the doorbell? Well, if it was, then someone else could get it. He was nowhere near. Seeing a man called Rick whom he knew from the campaign to save the school playing fields, he wandered over. 'So how are things with you, eh?'

'Strange bean stuff, this,' said Rick, prodding with a fork. (He had forgotten Barry was the host.) 'Tastes more like toast than beans.'

'That's probably because one of my lazy children forgot to stir it when the pinger went, so it got burned.'

Rick looked vaguely around him. 'So where are your kids, anyhow?'

Barry did not want to admit he didn't know. From the first ring on the doorbell, there'd been no sign of any of them. Ned, he could guess, would be holed up in his room, glued to some screen and slipping out from time to time to steal more crisps and Bombay mix. Lou would be hiding somewhere, no doubt being scathing on her phone to her mates about the guests' extraordinary costumes. And as for Lindy, she had probably slipped out through the back door and gone to Jade's house.

He might not know exactly where they were, but he knew them.

*

Tory thought, 'Someone will get it,' when she heard the doorbell ring. She'd had too much to drink to hurry down the stairs, and what Denise was telling her about her boss was far too interesting to miss. In any case, after an hour or two, guests at a party ought to be able to shift for themselves, and that included pushing open an unlocked front door if they arrived late, and pouring their own drinks.

She didn't try to work out who it was. Not much point, really. Sooner or later she would bump into them in one room or another. And she was not that keen on going down to the kitchen where the smell of burn still hung over everything. (Bloody Lou! Careless with anything that didn't matter to her!) So Tory sat tight, letting Denise moan on about her awful boss and just how spiteful some of the other people in her firm could be.

Now, bugger! Someone else was coming up the stairs, and either she or Denise would have to clamber upright to let them past. She was the hostess, so it should be her who made the gesture. Upsy-daisy, then! Now Tory knew for certain that she shouldn't have encouraged Barry to refill her glass. She felt quite dizzy. Leaning to the side, she let her forehead fall against the landing window. Cool, cool glass.

Was that her sister out there? Could it be? It looked like Megan, hurrying away across the grass. She couldn't see her car, though that meant nothing since the parking along the Crescent would be impossible tonight. But wasn't Megan supposed to be with Elinor this evening? Had something happened – some downturn in their mother's health? What awful luck, though, that her sister had come round to hear the music and see all the lights. As likely as not she'd even peered through the window and seen the guests in their mad Easter costumes.

That won't have helped. For one thing Megan would have realised that Tory had been fibbing when she said, 'Oh, no. Not a real party.' And it would also have reminded this touchy sister of hers of that grim moment when Megan hurried through her own kitchen doorway carrying a giant plate of sausages on sticks towards her guests, only to come face to face with Tory's flagrant mockery of herself and her unflattering style.

Oh, well! If it were something serious that had brought her sister round tonight, reminders of the past might fall away as totally unimportant. Should she ring Megan?

No. This was supposed to be a merry evening, for God's sake! And Elinor had been ill for months, draining everyone's crystals. So surely she and Barry had earned one Friday evening off. If it were something desperate, then Megan could pick up the phone herself. She knew that Tory's landline was still on the blink – something to do with an obsolete sort of handset battery. But since the last time Elinor came out of hospital Tory had made a special effort to keep her mobile near her, and well charged.

The damn thing must be somewhere.

Now, in the hall below, she could see Barry threading through the noisy throng linked arm in arm with two girls from his office, decked out alike in trailing green and yellow gowns. What were they? Daffodils? She ought to go and say hello to them. She'd spent so long with Denise that she'd neglected half the guests, and left poor Barry to do all the work.

Steadying herself against the window frame, Tory took a deep breath. 'Just a tick,' she told Denise. 'I really want to hear the rest, but right now I had better check there's still enough food out.'

Clutching the banister, she took the stairs with care and made her way down to the kitchen.

No fear of running out of food. The burned beans had been barely touched.

*

Megan found herself sweating with relief. Thank God that no one in that house had bothered to answer the door! At first she'd thought the dance music must have been pouring out from one of the children's bedrooms. But then she'd stepped sideways off the path and seen the group in the living room, two of them dressed as bunnies, a few with a crazy ribboned bonnets, and almost all the rest of them wearing bright yellow.

An Easter party, then. She'd turned and fled.

Once she was safely back in her car, she couldn't understand what madness had possessed her to take a detour to call in at Tory's house. Why would she ever have thought there might be something that her sister could have said or done to help the situation? Was it that peck on the cheek a few days before that led her to imagine Tory might sympathise with her predicament, and offer to lobby on her and Malcolm's behalf? 'I know! Barry and I will go round to Mum and tell her we feel terrible about the fact that we've ended up with so much more than you two.'

As Bethany would say, 'Sooo likely... Not!'

And what would Malcolm think when she got home? Would he assume she must have tackled the issue with her mother clumsily? Or not tried hard enough? In one way, Megan could see Elinor's point. What's spent is spent, and perhaps to an outsider it would look odd if she and Malcolm had a larger share in Elinor's will.

Until you understood the background of the case...

The case! Already it was sounding like a legal battle. But all she wanted was for Elinor to put things right and try to make up a little for the years of unfairness. Her mother couldn't just shrug the responsibility off onto Gordon and claim, 'Nothing to do with me.'

And Gordon's behaviour was a mystery. He must have been a very different man from the one she'd assumed she knew. Lord knows, she'd heard enough about the step-parents of her daughters' friends to know that some of them had very little patience with the foibles of the children into whose lives they'd stepped. They could be endlessly critical, forever urging firmness on the proper parent. (The 'proper' parent? Didn't that say it all!) Look at poor Cookie Henning in Amy's class. The head had even felt obliged to step in at one point, suggesting to Mrs Henning that it might be best if she took everyone now under her roof into some sort of family therapy.

There hadn't seemed to be so many strains in their own household. Yes, she'd been curt and rude to Gordon while she was growing up. Offensive, sometimes. She'd never warmed to him. But she had always thought that he was gentle and patient enough with her, and fair in his dealings. She'd never had the sense he hated her, or even wished her ill. She'd simply thought that he had tired of her hostile attitude, and learned to ignore her. No doubt her sister had been easier to love. But there again, it had been so much easier for Tory to care for Gordon. She'd barely even remembered their real dad.

So had things been a whole lot worse than she'd thought? Had Gordon had more of a say than Megan ever realised in some of the things she resented? Just take the business of her mother's irritation with her night-time grief. Had that, perhaps, been fuelled by Gordon? 'Don't indulge her, Elinor! She's only out to get attention. Just go in there and tell her to pack that stupid sobbing in, then come straight back to bed.'

Could that have been the way it was? She could remember knowing even at the time that she had often gone too far. Perhaps a level of unease at her own bad behaviour had blinded her to Gordon's faults.

Perhaps he'd been a quiet troublemaker all along.

6.

Malcolm was so incensed he couldn't settle. 'That's all your mother said? "All Gordon's doing. Nothing to do with me"?'

'That's about it.'

'And then she feigns a headache to get you out of there? My Christ! The nerve of it!'

'You can't believe how small I felt.' (She nearly added, 'I was so upset I went to Tory's,' but bit it back. With Malcolm in this mood there was no sense in setting more hares running.)

He bashed his fist into the palm of his hand. 'Why should she act like such a bitch? Even if she believes you have no reason to complain, she could still be polite.'

'I don't expect she's thinking much of other people's feelings now.'

He wasn't mollified by the idea of Elinor's approaching death. 'Well, even so…'

'I'm glad it's over, anyway.'

'It isn't, though,' he warned. 'No, not at all. Why should she get away with fobbing you off like that? I think she owes us both a better explanation than simply dumping everything on Gordon.'

She asked him nervously, 'What are you planning?'

'I'm going round there.'

'Now?'

'Of course not. Tomorrow, after I've dropped Amy off at her rehearsal. I'll just stop by the house and take a stab at getting Elinor to look at things in a more reasonable way.'

Suddenly Megan felt dead tired. 'Good luck with that, then.'

He drew her closer to him. 'Yes, I'm going to need it.'

'You certainly are.' She felt his fingers sliding up each of her nightgown sleeves. He loved a challenge. First her, tonight, though he knew perfectly well she couldn't have felt less like staying awake and making love. Then, in the morning, taking on her mother. On any other evening Megan would have fretted herself silly about what he might say to Elinor, how far he'd go. But right now she felt that Elinor could take her chances with Malcolm's determination and his arguments, even his temper. Why shouldn't she be made to feel a bit uncomfortable? She'd spooned out enough unpleasantness to Megan tonight, so she deserved a little of it in return.

*

After, while they were lying comfortably in one another's arms, she asked him, 'What are you going to say to her?'

He didn't want to be dragged out of his warm, happy fug of relaxation. 'Tell you tomorrow.'

'I know what I'd say,' she returned. 'I'd tell her that she can't just—'

There was his finger on her lips. 'Sssh!'

'No, it's a good point I'm making.'

'It doesn't matter, though. Because I won't be listening. I'm going to sleep. We'll talk about it in the morning.'

She thought she'd be awake the whole night long, inventing speeches in her brain, practising them over and over. 'And then you could tell her...', 'And don't forget to mention...' But when she rolled onto her side, the whole lot floated off. All that was in her mind was the loud music pouring out of Tory's house.

'*Just wanna dance the night away*
With señoritas who can sway...'

She was asleep in moments.

*

Next morning, Megan and Malcolm reached the printing works to find that two of the drivers had phoned in sick. Megan looked at the boxes to be delivered. 'Why don't I take the southern route? And Harry won't mind working round the rest, so long as he gets proper overtime.'

'Fair do's,' said Malcolm.

She left the car park at her usual lick. A forcible reminder of the van's primitive suspension came at the speed bump, so she settled down. It was an easy run to Petersbury, where the great bulk of stuff was dropped. The road across to Rosevale Heights was slow and tiresome, with roadworks every few miles. And the last place she had things to deliver, in a new building centre off the Harmire Road, was hard to find.

And yet by lunchtime she was done. On the road home, she saw a sign to Childon and, before she even realised she was signalling, branched off. It was a good few years since she had seen her father's grave. She

78

had brought Elinor one day, before some elderly aunts from Australia came over one last time to visit their childhood haunts. 'They're bound to want to see where John was buried,' Elinor had fretted. 'I think I ought to go and check it's in a reasonable state.'

It had looked quite neglected, so Elinor had set about it with a trowel while Megan drove back to the garden centre they had noticed on the road. 'Look for a climbing rose,' Elinor had suggested. 'Something with good roots that might take in time. That sort of thing.'

The errand sounded quick enough, but choosing took time, and Megan had to queue for twenty minutes simply to get to the till. On the drive back she'd been held up because two cars collided at a set of traffic lights, and though it was perfectly clear that no one had been hurt, some snotty officer was letting nothing past. By the time Megan had got back to the cemetery and dug in rose plant, Elinor was bored and impatient. 'I think we should be getting home.' Not even waiting for a word from Megan, she'd headed off towards the car. Megan had tried to take a moment to stand by her father's grave and think about him. But it was impossible.

This time, she left the van beside the road and went through the small lychgate. The sun was shining on the grave. The rose, of course, had died. Megan tugged up the shrivelled roots and tossed them on a heap of grass cuttings beside the fence. The stone seemed far, far smaller than she remembered. In Loving Memory of John Stuart Brown, then, underneath, the all-too-close-to-one-another dates of birth and death. As Megan stared, she suddenly recalled her father throwing chocolate beans into the air so she could try to catch them in her mouth. She almost felt the crunch between her teeth and tasted melting chocolate. Where had the two of them been at that moment? In some forgotten park? Surely not in that pocket handkerchief back garden. She'd have remembered that.

Beneath the weathered lettering was blank space, and for the first time ever Megan realised that it was there to take her mother's name when that day came. The freshly widowed Elinor would have been asked if this grave was intended to be shared, and no doubt before Gordon came along, that's what the world, including Elinor, would have assumed.

How odd, that things could slide away so quickly from what had been intended. For several weeks they had come to this place. She could remember Tory cartwheeling between the graves, her mother getting cross. 'Victoria! Stop that! It's not respectful!'

Had Megan stood and cried, the way she did at nights? Not that she could remember. In fact, this cemetery seemed much more linked to Elinor's grief than to her own. And so, once Gordon was on the scene, they'd barely come again – except maybe on her father's birthday, or some time round Christmas. Then Gordon had suggested the move to Tannington – the bigger house, the smarter school – and the visits to the cemetery were over. Megan remembered bringing Malcolm down to Childon once when they were courting. Both of the girls had seen it.

No one had ever bothered with another rose.

*

Malcolm had never really cared much for his mother-in-law. He thought her a cold fish. He had so many memories of his own mother, who had been plump and pink, and always dressed in brightly coloured frocks. She'd sailed through life dispensing humour and comfort along with endless cups of tea. Window cleaners, gas fitters, emergency electricians – they all extended their breaks to get a little longer in her company. Neighbours called round in droves. When she first let the world know just how ill she was, the house filled up with flowers, the freezer bulged with offerings, the phone was rarely quiet.

Compared to that, Elinor was stiff, unyielding, disapproving. He blamed her for his wife's social unease because he couldn't help but feel the same way in his mother-in-law's company – as if he wasn't quite up to scratch, or she knew something bad about him that she wasn't letting on.

He wasn't looking forward to the interview. But as he'd pointed out to Megan, what did they have to lose? Elinor wouldn't dare get cross enough to cut one of her daughters out of her will entirely. The worst that would happen, after he had explained their thinking, is that she'd think the two of them were being petty and grasping (and he could handle that). Or that she'd thwart him by putting off making any appointment with her solicitor to change things 'till she felt a little stronger', leaving things too late.

He certainly hadn't thought that she might argue. But she did. Forcing her frail body forward in the chair to check that the folds of her dressing gown were covering her legs, she said to him equably, 'As I told Megan last night, that was all Gordon's business. Nothing to do with me.'

Was hiding even the last inch of her ankles some defensive form of modesty? Or was she feeling cold? He'd been surprised to find her still not dressed at ten in the morning. Maybe she was a good deal weaker than they realised. He started gently. 'I'm not sure you can really say that, Elinor. After all, they are your daughters, and Gordon was your husband. So it's a little hard to believe you couldn't have had any say when things got so much out of kilter.'

She gave him one of those cool looks he so disliked. 'I think that Gordon always felt he had good reasons for the cheques he wrote. We always hoped that Tory and Barry would find a niche in life that suited them, instead of all these rather hand-to-mouth ventures.'

'I offered both of them positions more than once,' he couldn't help reminding her. 'But it was obvious they didn't want that sort of work.'

('Steady', is what he meant. The sort of jobs where you come in at the same time each morning and just get on with it.)

'No,' she said rather haughtily. 'I don't think that would have suited them at all.'

Now he was irritated. 'But don't you see? Megan and I put huge amounts of effort into making our business work. We slaved away all hours and made a lot of sacrifices. It doesn't seem at all right that those two should—' Oh, hell. Just spit it out. 'Why those two should have been indulged in what amounts to flakiness, at Megan's expense.'

She almost sniffed at him. 'You know inheritance is not a right.'

He fought back. 'Yes, but don't you think that fairness is a duty?'

'Only between honest people.'

That was a body blow. He stared at her. 'What do you mean?'

'Gordon had a godmother, you know. Her name was Edith Tallentire.' She offered Malcolm her most acid smile. 'I think you bought her cow byre.'

Cow byre? It was a moment or two before Malcolm caught on. That little agricultural stone shed had been their charming guest suite for so long that he had practically forgotten it was once a simple cow byre. But Elinor was still regarding him in that strange, spiteful and triumphant way. How had that little deal got anything to do with being honest?

Then he remembered.

Malcolm felt sick. Oh, Christ! Those little chats with James Harrow. All those years ago!

Lack of confidence between a married couple over the husband's dubious financial dealings.

Now she was struggling to her feet, preparing to dismiss him. 'I think there was some worry at the start that legal processes might cost a lot. But then it turned out it was simple after all. Wasn't that fortunate?' She pulled her dressing gown more tightly round her as she turned towards the door. 'I think the last thing Gordon ever wanted was to introduce a lack of confidence between a married couple over the husband's dubious financial dealings. Still, he never cared for—' Deliberately, she paused. 'That type.'

That type? He cringed.

She offered him one last malicious smile. 'Especially those who try to take advantage of the elderly. Gordon most particularly hated that.'

*

How the hell had they known? Who was it who could possibly have told the pair of them about that harmless little plan? It never came off anyway! It never happened! The cow byre had changed hands for a fair price, and the legalities had ended up being quite reasonable, and scrupulously shared between the two parties.

Surely that can't have been the reason Gordon never put his hand in his pocket after that to give them anything, and simply stuck to doling money out to Tory and Barry. Had he assumed that Megan knew about the little scam, and had approved it? What shitty luck, that old Miss Tallentire should turn out to have been Gordon's godmother! And how come he and Megan had never known that? After all, they'd chatted to the woman often enough when they met in the courtyard.

He pulled into a lay-by. For the first time in twenty years, Malcolm wished he still smoked. Before he faced his wife, he needed to work out how Gordon found him out. He couldn't believe that he and James Harrow ever discussed the business openly. He had no memory of ever mentioning it in James's office. It was the sort of thing they'd talk about during a game of golf, or as they strolled back to the bar. Who could have overheard them?

But clearly, someone had. And now he thought about it, hadn't the plan been quietly abandoned because it all became a little awkward? He scoured his memory. Something to do with some odd phone call to James's office that had put him enough on guard to back out of the plan.

He could phone up and ask if James remembered. No. Better not. No point in raking over that old ground. But he would have to think what he could say when he got home to Megan. She had been rather fond of Miss Tallentire – sent the girls round with cakes and scones, and even visited her in the nursing home till the old lady went so doolally that there was no real point. He wouldn't want to have to explain to Megan that Gordon had cut them off from all his generosity because he'd always known Malcolm had hoped to do a swindle on a sweet old lady.

Oh, bugger! Bugger! What to do?

Malcolm sat in the car for quite a while, chewing a hangnail and staring out over the countryside. He watched a cow scratching its flank against a barbed wire fence. 'You lucky bastard. Nothing to think about all day except your stomach.' He heard the traffic roaring past and tried to work out how he could spin this story so he would not sound like the villain Gordon and Elinor had obviously thought him.

But at least Elinor wouldn't split on him unless she were provoked, he could be sure of that. Oh, she'd enjoyed the panicked look on his face. But what she'd said about not introducing doubt between a husband and his wife had made it pretty clear that he was on safe ground. She'd just been making him back off, not planning to pursue him any further by feeding ugly truths to her daughter. If she had wanted to do that, she would have done it years ago.

He breathed out, feeling a tiny bit more confident. Elinor's discretion would give him more of a free hand. What could he say to Megan? He could pretend that he'd got nowhere in the interview, that Elinor had had fobbed him off, or claimed she was too tired to discuss the matter.

Or he could make up something that let him off the hook.

Yes, he could do that.

*

'She said what?'

Malcolm spread his hands. 'I know. It's unbelievable. Almost too hard to believe. But she admitted that Gordon always hated you.'

Megan went pale. 'Hated me? Mum put it as strongly as that? That Gordon actually hated me?'

God! Had he gone too far? No. No, he bloody hadn't. The man deserved it. All that guff through Elinor about, 'Gordon never cared for that type,' and, 'Gordon most particularly hated that.' Bleh, bleh. Bleh, bleh. So easy for the prosperous to feel contempt for others' ways of trying to build halfway as cosy a nest.

Still, Megan was looking shell-shocked. Dropping to his knees in front of her chair, Malcolm took her hands in his. 'Megan, your mother didn't want to say it. And she was clearly woozy from her drugs. She wasn't making total sense.' He launched into the part he had rehearsed over and over, to protect himself. 'And she did tell me she would only explain if I promised – truly, truly promised – never to pass it on to you. She didn't want you upset.'

'But Gordon has always hated me?'

He squeezed her hands. 'That was the gist of it. But Megan, you must swear to me that you won't bring it up with Elinor. She didn't want to tell me this. She was just doing me a favour, thinking that we deserved an explanation.'

'I can't believe it,' Megan said. And then again, 'I can't believe it.'

'It is extraordinary.' He took a punt. 'But she does plan to make amends. Your mother has every intention of sorting things out.'

'That's not what she said yesterday!'

'No. She was thrown into a bit of a state by what you said. And she was very torn. It's difficult for her, of course, not to think well of Gordon. After all, they were married all those years, and no one likes to think that they are hitched up to a vengeful bastard.' He felt an extra stab of guilt as he came out with that one, and hurried back to the script he now had pat. 'And so I promised her – promised her faithfully – that you would never raise the topic with her again. She says she just can't bear it. It's too painful. All that she wants is for the two of you to carry on as if things are dead fair. Meanwhile, she's going to do her level best to sort it out. She's going to count up what was given to them, and get the will changed so it all sorts out.'

'But I'm not to talk to her about it? Not at all? Not even to thank her?'

'Not even to thank her! She especially said that. I think she reckons that she's somehow being unfaithful to Gordon by even considering changing her will so it no longer is the same as his.'

Megan said eagerly, 'That's certainly the feeling I had when I spoke to her. She didn't want to go against his wishes.'

'Yes.' Once again, Malcolm squeezed her hands. 'So you do promise not to say a word?'

She still looked baffled. 'I suppose so.'

'No,' he said firmly. 'There's to be no supposing. It was a difficult morning for me, and I made promises – serious promises – on your behalf. So you must swear to me that you will keep them.' He stood up. 'After all, your mother is a dying woman.'

'Yes,' Megan said thoughtfully. 'She's dying.'

'And pretty soon, I think. I must say, she looked horribly frail this morning. So it's important that we don't upset her last few weeks. I know that you might want to know a whole lot more about what went through Gordon's mind – why he should be so mean and unforgiving. But I have promised her that you won't bring it up. So you won't, will you?'

She looked into his face. All she could see was honest love for her, and care and concern for her poor dying mother.

'It won't be easy. I'd really like to know why he could be so hateful – and so adamant. But if you promised her…'

'I did. I really did.'

She sighed. 'All right, then. Since she's so very sick…'

'There's a good girl,' he said. And she was still so shocked by what she'd heard, she didn't even hear the patronising phrase that would have maddened her at any other moment in their marriage.

*

It ate away at Megan. She had agreed to say nothing to Elinor, but she still wanted to know more from him. 'What did she say, exactly?'

He thrashed around, desperate to recall snippets of stories she had told him in the past. 'That time you hid his car keys just before he had an important meeting. Oh, yes. And something about deliberately spilling perfume over something.'

'His favourite tie. It stank so badly that he had to throw it out.'

He reckoned he was doing well, and took a chance on one more thing he half recalled her telling him some years before. 'At one point she said something about a school prize-giving night. I can't remember any of the details.'

'I can,' she said. 'I told them there were so few seats that we were only allowed to invite one parent each. So Mum came, then she noticed all the others were in pairs, and even threes or fours if there were step-parents. She probably wouldn't have mentioned it to him, so he would never have known except that he had driven us to the school and then came back to pick us up. The moment we were in the car he said to me sarcastically, "There must be dozens of parents in your school having affairs, if you can judge by all those couples coming down the steps." And then, the moment we were back in the house, she sent me up to bed.'

'I suppose that kind of thing can rankle.'

'I suppose so. Especially if you're trying to worm your way into someone's affections and they won't have it.' After a moment, Megan added bitterly, 'And what with Tory rolling over and adoring him right from the start, I must have seemed so stubborn, still to be giving him the big freeze four or five years later.'

'Perhaps your mother should have thought about your feelings before she roped Gordon in to live with you.'

'She hated being alone. It made her feel a failure.'

'My mother managed it.'

'So did the mothers of a lot of people in my school. But Elinor's not the type. She needs a man to lean on, and take responsibility for everything.' A thought struck Megan. 'Maybe that's why her health is taking such a dive – because she's all alone now and just can't stand it.'

'She's not that much alone,' he pointed out. 'The two of you make endless visits, and you've both invited her to come and live with you.'

She shrugged. 'Well, I can understand her not wanting to move into Tory's house. It's so chaotic and noisy.'

'And grubby.'

'Grubby, yes. And Mum hates that. She's always been tremendously fastidious about clean knives and shining surfaces.'

He saw his chance to get away, 'Speaking of shining surfaces, I promised that I'd get your car done, so I'll do that now.'

He fled the room, leaving his wife to think a little longer about her mother. Had she not minded the ill-feeling in the house? They had been mired in it – year after year of Megan's sulks and petty acts of spite, and after that, it seemed, a matching period of quiet, firm revenge on Gordon's part. How had Elinor stood it?

Self-discipline, presumably. And really wanting not to be alone. Wasn't that how abuse cases begin, when women hang their heads in court and can't explain how they have let their boyfriend torment their child, except to say, 'I worried he would leave if I said anything.'

A thought struck Megan. Elinor had rid the house of everything of Gordon's within a fortnight of his death! His ashes had been barely cold before she had insisted on every last item that reminded her of him being removed. She had been so precipitous about it that even Mrs Deloy had thought it odd, and dared remark on it. Could that, thought Megan, have been some unconscious stab at reparation for the patience that Elinor now realised she'd shown too much of before? Was it a sign she never had, at heart, approved of Gordon's unspoken but determined financial retaliation against Megan?

Had that unhappy, grieving daughter truly been loved by Elinor after all?

*

While Tory and Megan sat side by side outside the doctor's office, Tory said suddenly, 'There's something I meant to ask you. The Friday before last, did you come round to our house? I could have sworn that I saw someone who looked just like you walking across our lawn.'

Lawn, indeed! Megan hid her smile. Tory and Barry had the scrappiest patch of grass in the whole of Staines Crescent. 'No, that can't have been me. That was the night you had a couple of friends for supper, wasn't it? I was at Mum's.'

'That's right. Because we swapped. But I forgot to do my visit on the Saturday.'

'Hung-over?'

Tory offered her a smile. Megan was so easy today. She reckoned that her sister must be changing personality before her very eyes. They had sat here for nearly twenty minutes now without a single niggle.

After a while, Tory got restless. 'What's going on in there, do you suppose? Just more of their endless tests?'

'I wonder why she didn't want us to go in with her.'

'Perhaps she thought three was a crowd and couldn't choose between us.'

'Yes, probably.' Megan stuck her legs out to inspect her shoes. 'You'd have been better at it, anyway. You always seem to manage to keep things lighter, even when they're desperate.'

'Do you believe they are?'

'Desperate?' Megan nodded. 'Yes, I suppose I do now. She's started getting quite confused. Mrs Deloy says Mum was filling the laundry basket last week with a heap of stuff she'd only just ironed. And she says Elinor keeps trying to give the carers cash, even though she's been told a dozen times that isn't how it works.'

'Oh, God.'

'And she's so thin. She must have lost a huge amount more weight. She barely has the strength to prise herself out of her chair.'

'Perhaps we ought to buy her one of those fancy affairs where you can press a button to get yourself tipped forward,' suggested Tory.

'Renting one would be far more sensible,' said Megan. She turned to see her sister staring at her in astonishment. 'Well,' she defended herself, 'it would.'

'Yes,' Tory said. 'It's just I would never have expected you to say it first.'

'Why not?'

But Tory wasn't going to risk upsetting their new companionability. 'Oh, I don't know. I suppose, what with Malcolm's father being dead so long, and his Mum going so fast, I didn't think you were so up to speed on all this sort of thing.'

But Megan had stopped listening and gone off on another tack. 'She won't be able to stay home very much longer – not unless she takes to her bed and we get even more people to come in.'

'She'd prefer that to any hospital ward.'

'I doubt if it will be on offer. It seems to me the choice is going to be between a nursing home and a hospice.'

'Christ!' Tory said. She couldn't help it. All of a sudden, from resisting every single hint that Elinor's case was hopeless, Megan was racing ahead and practically had their mother dead and buried. She stole another glance at her surprising sister. What could have happened in the last few days to cause this transformation?

Once again Megan caught her staring. 'Problem?' she asked.

'No,' Tory told her hastily. 'I was just wondering if you would think me a huge pig if I went down to that machine again to get more chocolate.'

'You go ahead,' said Megan. 'I'll hold the fort.'

*

Inside the bright white room, Elinor struggled to sit up again. The nurse put out an arm to steady her, then lifted both her legs to swing them round. 'Are you all right, Mrs Forsyth? Not feeling too dizzy?'

Elinor shook her head. She felt so fuzzy all the time now on the painkillers that being dizzy scarcely registered.

The doctor swivelled back from putting something into the computer. 'All finished, Elinor. I'm sorry if that was a bit uncomfortable. I did try not to linger.'

Elinor dimly felt obliged to reassure her, but her throat was far too dry for speech. Nurse Connaught heard the little rasping noise and crossed the room to fetch a cup of water from the dispenser by the door.

Dr Nagpal stood studying Elinor for a moment before she came out with the verdict. 'Not looking any better, I'm afraid. And obviously you're very, very tender.' She didn't wait for Elinor to ask her questions. She just hurried on. 'I'm going to start you on some different painkillers. You'll find they work much better, but you'll need something else to keep them down. So what I'm going to do is—'

Elinor stopped listening. What was the point? She did what she was told. She had what little Ellie (who now came in twice a day, and not just once) called a 'dosette' box. Days of the week were marked, and each of the sections was divided into lidded compartments. Morning pills, lunchtime pills, late afternoon pills and the final bedtime pills. You'd have to be an idiot to get it wrong.

Or woozy with the stuff that you had taken hours before. Why not stop all of it? Just flush the whole lot down the lavatory. Be done with trying.

Better still maybe, take all the painkillers and be done with life.

Odd! She'd never thought about that possibility. While Dr Nagpal droned on about someone coming round to talk about a change in the 'care plan', Elinor, for the first time in her life, thought about suicide. Whenever she and Gordon discussed the various drawn-out, miserable ways their friends were dying, he'd claimed that jumping off a building before dawn would be the best way. 'Nobody on the streets. No changing your mind halfway through. Certain to work.'

The idea gave her shudders. But painkillers – they were a different matter. The girls would understand – certainly Tory would. In fact, her younger daughter was the sort who'd probably help her out. Give her advice. Go on some website to find out what you had to take along with an overdose of pills to keep them down. Whisky. Or ice cream. Elinor could recall reading about it – one of those articles in which people write about the most astonishingly private matters simply to get into print. Yes, careless as she was in every other way, if you asked Tory how to kill yourself efficiently, and without pain, she wouldn't raise an eyebrow and she'd come up trumps.

Not Megan, though. My God! If somebody asked Megan to do so much as pick up two weeks of prescription drugs instead of one, she'd turn all snippety. 'I don't think I should do that.' How could two girls end up so different in every way, the first so buttoned-up, the second one so easy-come, easy-go?

But maybe that was because things had been easy for Tory. Not just losing her father at such a young age she barely noticed it. But things coming so smoothly after that. Just bright and merry enough to get away with slovenliness in school. Unthinking enough to be excused each outrage. 'Oh, that's just Tory for you!' Why, even the shocking way she had sloped off to marry without a word had been forgiven quite astonishingly soon, almost as if you couldn't reasonably expect anything more of Tory than simple self-absorption. Though Megan more than once had pointed out that—

Who was that tapping on her knee? Nurse Connaught. Dr Nagpal was still rabbiting on. 'So you'll give it some thought?'

Elinor forced herself to pay attention long enough to answer, 'About the painkillers?'

'No,' Dr Nagpal said. 'About St Bride's.'

St Bride's? That was a hospice, wasn't it?

Yes. She was sure of it. Yes, yes it was.

7.

Barry had never had a phone call from Malcolm before. He didn't even know how Malcolm found his number (though it was not polite to ask). He had been fooling about with Alexandra in the office, snatching away her papers, then offering them back, just flirting with her, wasting time on yet another afternoon with almost nothing to do. (How long would they keep him? No more than a month or two, that was for sure.)

The minute he heard his brother-in-law's voice, Barry was on his mettle. 'You want to talk?'

'If you don't mind... Perhaps just the two of us? Tiny bit awkward.'

'I see.' (Though he didn't.) Making apologetic faces at Alexandra, he backed out of the office into the corridor where there was nobody about. 'Did you mean now?'

'When do you get away?'

Barry could have laughed aloud. He hadn't had a proper client all day. But best to keep one's end up in the family. 'It doesn't matter, really. My time is basically my own.'

It was quite obvious that Malcolm had thought this through. 'That place below your office – what's it called? Harvey's?'

'Howey's.'

'Shall we meet there? Ten minutes, say?'

Ten minutes? That meant that Malcolm must already be near. What sort of mess could he be in? 'All right. Ten minutes, down in Howey's Bar. That'll suit me.'

'Excellent. I'll see you there.'

*

Malcolm was standing at the bar when Barry got there. 'What do you fancy?'

'Pipers Original. Half, please,' said Barry.

'So not the usual, then?' the girl behind the bar teased.

'What is the usual?' Malcolm asked Barry, curious.

'The full pint,' Barry admitted.

'It is your local, I suppose,' said Malcolm in forgiving tones. He carried the glasses to a side table, leaving the girl behind the bar to keep the last of the change.

'So what's your problem?' Barry asked, hoping to seize back the initiative.

Malcolm did not waste time. 'It's about Megan. It's about this will.'

'Gordon's?'

'No, Elinor's.'

'Oh.' Barry was startled, and a little disappointed. He had, he realised, been assuming that Malcolm wanted help to cover some transgression. Maybe an affair? Certainly something in the sleaze line, for why else would the man have made the effort to get in touch and, once he was in contact, arrange to meet at once? Always before, their meetings had been things to do with family, and planned by Elinor and Gordon or the sisters. Right from the start the brothers-in-law had not been close.

Better show willing, though. 'Elinor's Last Will and Testament? How can I help with that? Not even sure what's in it.'

Trust Malcolm to have the essence of its contents off pat. 'It is essentially the same as Gordon's. A tranche of money to each of the grandchildren, and the remainder split equally between Megan and Tory.'

'Sounds fair enough,' Barry said bravely, dreading a lecture on the extra legacy.

'Except it isn't,' Malcolm said. And off he went, not even bothering to mention Ned as a third child, but detailing, so far as he was able, the details of the extra money that had come Tory and Barry's way over the years. Then, sensing Barry's burgeoning humiliation at what amounted to a litany of his financial failures, hastily Malcolm moved on. 'The thing is, Megan's terribly upset. She won't say a word to her mother. But she does feel that Elinor should try to even all the payments out a bit in her own will.'

'What, give the pair of you a great wodge more?'

Malcolm put on a lofty look, as if the base mechanics of the problem hadn't occurred to him. 'I suppose so. No need to make it totally equitable, perhaps, but there should be a solid gesture. I do know how much that would comfort Megan, and make her feel less second-best.

But you know Elinor. She always left the finances to Gordon, so she'll need some persuasion.'

'And you think only me and Tory can put things right? So you want me to talk to Tory about it.'

'That's about it. If you don't mind.'

'No, I don't mind. I don't know what she'll think, but I can ask her.' Barry tipped back the last of his drink. 'Fancy another?'

'I should be getting back.' As they were leaving, Malcolm laid a hand on Barry's arm. 'You will tell Tory not to say a word about me prompting you on this?'

'To Elinor? Or Megan?'

'To either. You see, if Elinor finds out, she might get stubborn. You know. Residual loyalty to Gordon, who never cared much for me. And if Megan gets to hear about it, things will be worse. She'll just be even more upset because her mother didn't sort things out spontaneously.'

Barry could not help grinning. 'If Elinor sorts them out at all.'

Malcolm's pained grimace in no way matched his cheery laugh. 'Oh, well. We can but try.'

And that is what I've done, he told himself on the drive home. I've tried. I've given it my best shot and can do nothing more. Now I must trust to luck.

*

Tory was panicking. 'She isn't anywhere! I've phoned around. She's not at Jade's, and Jade says she has no idea where Lindy might be. It seems they had a quarrel a few days ago, and have barely spoken since. She told me Lindy has a new friend now. Someone called Esther. Christ knows where Esther lives! And Jade claimed that she didn't know if Lindy was even in school today.'

'How could she not know? They're in the very same classes!'

'She says she "didn't notice". Maybe she was acting cool. But when I rang the school, all I got was the answer phone.' Tory scowled. 'Idlers! All of those teachers out of there well before five, I noticed!'

He tried to make a joke of it. 'We should have sent her to St Hilda's. I bet they keep on answering the phone to worried parents till at least ten at night.'

But Tory wasn't listening. 'I hadn't realised!'

'About the fact she wasn't here last night? Why should you? After all, she has been practically living over at Jade's house.'

Tory went ashen. 'Barry! Did she sleep here on Tuesday, even?'

He panicked too, for a moment. And then he said, 'Yes. Yes, she did. Because she had that blazing row with Ned about the fact that he'd changed settings on her phone. And I remember that because I was trying to watch Tottenham play Stoke.'

Anxiety did nothing for Tory's temperament. 'Oh, yes! If it's to do with football, you remember it.'

'Don't pick on me because you're worried.'

'You could at least do something, and not just stand there. Can't you phone someone?'

'Who?'

'I don't know.' Tory glanced at the wall clock that had been stopped for weeks, then at her watch. 'Is it too early to phone the police and tell them she's missing?'

'Tory! We don't even know for sure that Lindy was off school today! And even if she didn't go, it wouldn't be the first time she's bunked off.'

'I'm going to phone Jade again. Insist she tells us whether Lindy was there or not. And if she refuses, I'm going to ask to speak to her mother. That'll sort the little madam out.'

'Jade doesn't have a mother. You know that.'

'Do I?'

'Of course you do. You said you thought her father was a dish, and now the wife was gone you reckoned half the PTA would queue up to post home-baked scones through his letterbox.'

'Did I say that? When?'

'Ages ago.'

'So Lindy has been sleeping over at a house with just Jade and that father?'

'And his new girlfriend, Sue.'

'And what's she like, for fuck's sake?'

'Tory, you've met her! She's the tall, chirpy one who drives the Audi convertible.'

'That one? She's just a teenager!'

'Don't be ridiculous. You're getting worked up about nothing here.'

'Don't fucking tell me what to get worked up about!'

The back door opened. Lindy strolled into the kitchen, pulling her brand new woolly out of shape around her. 'It's fucking freezing out there!'

'You watch your language,' Tory told her automatically.

Lindy studied their faces. 'Are you two having a row?'

'No,' Tory said.

'What's it about?'

'Mind your own business,' said Barry, and walked away. He didn't feel like telling Tory anything about his meeting with Malcolm. Leave it for another time.

Bad tempered witch.

*

Looking back afterwards, Barry assured himself that it was hardly surprising he hadn't rushed to revisit, either in his own mind, or openly with his wife, a conversation with his brother-in-law that had featured so many of his failures.

And the whole hour in Howey's had, frankly, been a little dull. Not that he wasn't used to that, of course, with Malcolm. Practically every Christmas when they met, they'd find themselves together in a corner, and Malcolm would begin to talk about where shares were going, or some such. It hardly meant a thing to Barry. Any loot he and Tory ever laid their hands upon was spent at once. But on the one or two occasions when he had tried to twist the conversation round to something more interesting, he'd simply found himself bored in another way.

'…come in on work experience, and then you have to explain to them for ten days in a row that keeping a floor clear of waste paper does mean exactly that: keeping it clear.'

'…but once you take into account the very fast depreciation…'

'…simply not up to scratch, and the girls in the workshop hated it. So in the end we traded up to the new Vandor XT 6 and everyone was a lot happier.'

Brain-frying stuff. So Barry had become quite used to simply thinking his own thoughts, nodding from time to time, and playing the professional wool-gatherers' trick of now and then repeating the last words spoken.

'…making them far less tax-efficient.'

'Less tax-efficient, yes.'

So had he even really grasped what Malcolm was on about? He thought he had. Megan (for whom no doubt read both of them) was pissed off that her stepfather had funded Barry and Tory's painted furniture plan, and one or two other projects along the way. So to make up for it she wanted more of Elinor's money when she died. But she was far too prissy to ask her mother directly. She wanted her sister to do it.

Simple. He would let Tory know when she was in a better mood. Or when he was himself.

*

It came to mind again a couple of days later. The two of them were leaning on a fence, watching poor constipated Archie going round in circles, desperately trying to crap.

'Get on with it,' Tory kept shouting at the dog. She rooted in her pockets for a poop bag. 'Can we go home now?'

'He hasn't managed yet. Nothing came out.'

'What on earth's wrong with him?' She sighed. 'Another bloody vet's bill. This is the last dog ever.'

'Until we're rich.' And that reminded him. 'Speaking of money, I never told you what happened on Thursday afternoon. You see—'

But she'd already interrupted him. 'Oh, Christ! Thursday! I never told you about Esther!'

'Esther?'

'Lindy's new friend. The one who's put Jade's nose so out of joint. It seems the reason Lindy didn't come home that night was that she felt she ought to stay with Esther, to comfort her because she's been suspended from school until there's been a disciplinary hearing.'

'What the hell's that? It sounds as serious as a court martial.'

'It is quite serious. Lindy thinks Esther's actually going to be permanently excluded.'

'Expelled, is that? What did she do?'

'Spat at the French teacher.'

'Spat?'

'So it seems. Anyway, the girl's in deep shit now.'

Both of them turned as if on cue, in time to see Archie succeed at his haunch-clenching labours. 'Thank God for that!'

On the way home, they talked about the lack of discipline in schools, the way that spitting had come back in fashion, and Archie's bowels.

And when they came through the door, it was to find that one of Ned's nosebleeds had left the usual trail across the kitchen, over the hall rugs, and onto the living room carpet.

'For Christ's sake!' Tory yelled. 'How many times have we told you not to drip blood on the carpets!'

Barry chimed in. 'And, like that doctor said, if you would just stop excavating up there with your fingers, these sodding nosebleeds wouldn't happen at all!'

In all the fuss of arguing about the clearing up, Barry forgot to pick up the story of his meeting with Malcolm. And Tory didn't know enough about it to ask.

*

Elinor dreaded Megan's next visit quite as much as Megan dreaded making it. But in the end it worked out well. Both of them started off as if they were treading on eggshells. 'How are you, darling? And how are the girls?'

'Never mind them, Mum. They're both fine. The question is, how are you?' Megan hung up her coat and peered in her shopping bag. 'I have a carrot cake and a fruit salad. I didn't know what you'd be feeling like, so I bought both. Which do you fancy?'

'You know, I do believe I'd love the tiniest splash of fresh fruit salad.'

'I thought you might.'

They settled easily and talked of this and that. The weather, obviously. Then Elinor's health. 'How is the pain?'

'These new pills work a whole lot better than the last, though I must say they make me very woozy. I'm used to walking into rooms and thinking, "Why did I come in here?" But now I can be holding the butter knife in one hand, a slice of toast in the other, and still have to make an effort to remember what I'm about.'

'You're doing very well. I am amazed at how you're coping.' Megan glanced round the room. It all looked clean and tidy. 'What about Mrs Deloy? She's coming in more often?'

'She's very kind. So are the carers. There is one who won't stir her stumps, and does the minimum. But I have asked the agency not to send her anymore.'

'Which one is that?'

Elinor tried to think. The name was in there somewhere, but it wouldn't come. Hastily, Megan moved on. 'So is there anything that Tory and I can do to make things easier? Anywhere you feel like going? Out for a spin, perhaps? We're no more busy than usual. Malcolm could manage without me and the car is very comfortable.'

Elinor waved the idea away. 'No, not this week, dear. I'm a little tired.'

'That visit to the hospital won't have helped.'

Elinor closed her eyes. Was Megan going to ask her what was said during that horrid check-up? Should she confess the name 'St Bride's' had passed Dr Nagpal's lips?

No. Leave all that for now. Elinor only said, 'They're very good. They couldn't be more kind.' The two of them went on to talk of some documentary about drunken girls that Elinor had watched the night before. And very soon, it seemed to Megan, the clock said half past five, and she could go.

*

To her surprise, Malcolm was already home. As she walked through the door he came across to take her coat. 'How was the visit?'

Megan was touched by his concern. 'It went just fine. Better than usual, in fact.'

'Really?'

'Yes. She was very easy.'

'What did you talk about?'

'Oh, you know. This and that.'

'But what, exactly?' He was studying her face. She guessed he might think she was hiding her concern, so made an effort to remember. 'You know. Weather. Fruit salads. Telly programmes. The carers.'

He couldn't help it. 'Nothing about the will?'

Oh, she was sick of all that. 'No. Nothing about the will. Or Gordon.' She changed the subject firmly. 'Are both the girls back? Are they doing homework?'

Bethany's finished hers. She's trawling about on her phone now.'

'How long's she been at that?'

'No more than half an hour.'

'We'll give her a tiny bit longer. And after that, supper and music practice.'

He knew that tone, so standing at the bottom of the stairs, he called up, 'Last ten minutes, Bethany!'

Their daily life was back on track. If Tory came up trumps and he was lucky, he might be home and dry.

*

Tory slung on her old fringed jacket. 'I'm off to Mum's now. It's my turn today.'

Mention of Elinor finally triggered memory. 'Oh, God. Hang on. I was supposed to tell you something.'

'What?'

'Malcolm wants you to do them a favour.'

'Malcolm?'

'Yes. He came round.'

'Here?'

'No. To my place at work. Well, not exactly. We met in the bar below.'

'You never told me. When was this?'

He searched his brain. 'Thursday, I think. It was that night that we were worried about Lindy, so it went out of my mind. And then I meant to tell you yesterday, but got distracted cleaning up after the nosebleed.'

Tory still had her hand on the back door knob. 'So why did he arrange to meet you? What did he want?'

Malcolm had not approached the matter with much tact. So why, thought Barry, should he put the case with any enthusiasm. 'The usual. Money, of course. He's on about the will being unfair.'

'That stupid business of the extra legacy for Ned?'

Barry did not see that he was obliged to detail Malcolm's estimates of money he and Tory had received – and dribbled away – over the last few years. So he restricted himself to saying only, 'Oh, I suppose so. And one or two other things, maybe.'

'That money for the jojoba?'

'That sort of thing.'

'But that was ages ago! And it was hardly anything.'

'I know. But he wants you to plead Megan's cause for her.'

Tory was irritated. 'With Mum? Why can't Megan plead it herself?'

'Too prissy, I suppose.'

'So I'm supposed to make an effort to do us out of money that we need and those two don't?'

'That's about it.'

'Ha!' Tory said, and left the house.

8.

Once she was with her mother it occurred to her that she should say something, otherwise Megan and Malcolm would be able to claim she'd had her own interests in mind. 'Mum, can I talk to you about the will?'

'Gordon's?'

'No, yours.'

'Oh, dear.'

Tory quite understood. 'I know. It's very tiresome. But Megan's got her knickers in a twist about it. Thinks that it isn't fair.' Seeing her mother's face set hard at once, Tory felt her first stab of sympathy for her resentful sister. And what would be the problem anyway in taking a high-minded line? How much would she and Barry truly be out of pocket if the children's legacies were evened up? Not much. There would be plenty left to be divided. 'So I was wondering if things might be a little easier…'

'You think I ought to change the will?'

'Megan would feel a whole lot better, that's for sure.'

'I suppose she would. Well, dear, thank you for telling me.'

Tory watched Elinor's fingers writhe in her lap. 'No problem, Mum,' she soothed. 'And any time you want me to hurl another chunk of my inheritance towards Miss Sourpuss, just say the word.'

It was a joke, but Tory instantly regretted it. The moment that her mother laughed, she crumpled up in pain. 'Oh, Tory!'

'God! I'm sorry!'

Tory was on her knees, her arms round Elinor. But it was a good long while before the extra painkillers she made her mother swallow had the slightest effect.

*

That night the pain was so bad that Elinor slept only in fits and starts. Occasionally her brain cleared just enough for her to go back to feeling troubled by what Tory had said. Should she phone the solicitor and get the will changed after all? She didn't want to think that Gordon was wrong in any way. But maybe he had been a little harsh with Malcolm and Megan, always refusing to offer them a single penny because of that strange business with Miss Haversham.

No. Not Miss Haversham. That was Great Expectations. Miss Tallentire.

And maybe Megan never had been in on that potential scam. Gordon was so furious, he didn't care. And she herself had never felt the urge to argue with him. After all, Megan and Malcolm were doing very well by then. Plenty of money. There was no need for Elinor to make a fuss about the fact that cheques went out to Tory all the time. Megan had that swish car. Her girls were in a private school. She never asked for money. Where was the problem?

But clearly things were different now. And if she didn't make some sort of effort to put things right, she'd leave ill-feeling behind her. It might be difficult for Tory, too. Whenever Megan got in one of her snits, she could be difficult. Elinor would like to think that both her girls could still think warmly of her after she was dead. And stay in touch with one another. No one had ever claimed the two of them had much in common, but they had always managed to stay friends in a strange, slightly formal way. She'd hate to think that their relationship would fall apart because of anything she'd done, or failed to do.

Yes, Tory was right. And she would not have brought the topic up if she'd not thought it was important. Nobody wants to talk to someone who is dying about their will. Well, maybe Malcolm had. But he was not the issue here. It was her daughters she was worried about. Only her daughters.

Oh, Lord! The cramps! She'd take tomorrow morning's pills right now.

As Elinor reached out to the dosette box, she felt a little ping inside her brain. It sounded like two tiny threads of Velcro being ripped apart. Her vision blurred, then mercifully cleared again, apart from some strange patch high on one side where she seemed suddenly to see things through a slippery, shimmering stream of ice.

No. Don't do anything in case it was a little stroke. Just lie there quietly. Try to ignore the pain.

*

Next morning, she felt better. She had intended to ask Tory to make an appointment at the solicitor's office. The two of them would go together. Then she remembered an occasion when one of Gordon's financial advisers came to the house. There were some papers to be signed – something to do with trusts or pensions.

Why shouldn't a solicitor make a home visit too? They must have housebound clients. And she'd prefer to do this without her daughters – either of them – peering over her shoulder. She'd ring and ask. The number would be in the book in the desk drawer. Yes, there it was. Russell Powers Solicitors. Tannington 634211.

She started on the number, but the code for Tannington slid from her brain. Strange, that. She'd known that code for decades. But now she had to look it up, then check it over and again while her stiff fingers picked their way through what appeared to have become a fog of numbers.

Finally she got it right. The woman who picked up the phone was helpful, offering several dates. But after Elinor explained that she was suffering from good and bad days, the secretary switched tack. 'So how's today, then? Is this good or bad?'

Elinor said, 'I'm feeling fuggy, but I think today is good.'

'Right, then. Why don't I send our Mrs Hatcher round? She only joined us recently, so has a few free times in her work diary.'

'But she is qualified? She'll get it right?'

'She's very experienced indeed,' the woman assured her. 'She's only come to us because her husband's job was moved.'

So it was all agreed. Mrs Hatcher would come round that morning.

To mark the small achievement, Elinor took another pill.

*

Mrs Hatcher arrived within the hour. Elinor, whose morning was turning out not quite so good as she had hoped, asked Mrs Deloy to leave the front door ajar. Mrs Hatcher tapped on it gently even though she was sure that Elinor had spotted her coming up the path. Then she walked in.

She was appalled at how pale and shaky her new client looked, and took the duties of a hostess on herself. 'It's very nice to meet you, Mrs Forsyth. Can I get you a cup of tea or anything, before we settle down?'

Elinor shook her head automatically, then changed her mind. 'Actually, tea would be lovely.' She watched as Mrs Hatcher laid her files and clipboard neatly on the table. Then she remembered. 'Oh, yes! You don't know where things are. You'll find the tea bags in a small blue china jar. The kettle's right beside it, and if you take milk, it's in a small white jug tucked in the door of the fridge.'

Right then, thought Esme Hatcher. She's of sound mind. (Last minute will changes could be an awkward issue if there were any doubts.)

By the time she came back into the living room carrying the tray she'd found stored upright by the stove, Elinor looked better. Mrs Hatcher poured. 'I hope that draught through the front door won't have left you with a chill.'

'I'm well beyond bothering about small things like chills, dear.'

Esme pulled her chair closer. These were the sorts of interviews at which she felt she excelled. She was forthcoming and yet sensitive. 'I've had a bit of a canter through your current will,' she said, tapping the envelope. 'I see you've kept it simple – a legacy for each grandchild, and then the rest split equally between your daughters.'

She waited. Elinor was silent, staring into space.

'So,' Esme prompted, 'I was wondering what you would like to change.'

She had to say it twice. The second time, Elinor pulled herself together. 'I am sorry. These painkillers make me so woozy that I tend to lose track.'

'That's all right. Plenty of time. Let's start with the grandchildren. Did you want to alter the amounts?'

'No, dear. I think I'd like to get rid of all those legacies completely.'

'Really?'

'Yes,' Elinor told her firmly. 'I'm afraid that they've caused a bit of trouble in the family, what with one of my daughters having more children than the other.' While Esme sat imagining a horde of offspring in one house, and one lonely waif in the other, Elinor carried on. 'I think it will be safer if I just split the estate between my daughters, and leave the business of the grandchildren to them.'

Esme was wary. 'There can be real disadvantages in—'

Elinor didn't care. 'No. It'll be easier. They'll have to sort it out themselves. I don't want any ill-feeling after I'm gone, and this is the way I think it will work out best.'

Esme said soothingly, 'Then that's the way we'll do it, Mrs Forsyth. Forget the legacies for all the grandchildren, and just divide the rest.'

She made a note. Elinor shifted uncomfortably, then braced herself to tackle the root of the matter. 'But I'm afraid things are even more complicated than that because, over the years, my late husband happened to give one of the girls a good deal of money. Huge amounts, in fact.' Elinor sighed. 'I never realised that it was an issue…' Again, she drifted into space as Esme Hatcher tried to disguise the wait by sipping tea. Then, wincing, she was back. 'Where were we?'

'You were explaining to me how Mr Forsyth had given more to one of the girls.'

'Yes, well, he did,' Elinor snapped, as if Mrs Hatcher had been arguing. 'And it has caused a bit of trouble.'

'And you would like to square things up?'

'I would.'

'So how much was involved in this discrepancy?'

Elinor had spent half the night trying to work it out. But she had never been much good at money. In the end she'd simply guessed. Now, to be safe, she doubled the amount.

Esme hid her astonishment, and only said, 'That much?'

'I think so.'

'We could try checking,' Esme suggested cautiously. 'I think a good deal of your late husband's paperwork is still in the office.'

Elinor waved away the idea of delay. 'No. Let's just say that it was that much and be done.'

'Whatever you think best.' Mrs Hatcher made another note. Then she trod delicately. 'But with things no longer being quite as balanced as before, would it be better not to keep your girls as joint executors? I was just thinking that might open the door to—' How should she put it tactfully? '—a bit of ill-feeling?'

Elinor tried to think. Tory had seemed content enough about the alteration – even suggested it. But there'd been spats between the girls before. And frosty periods. Perhaps it would be wiser to give them both a little space.

'So you'd suggest…?'

'Perhaps our Mr Douglas and our Miss Holloway? After all, your late husband was content with them.'

'Mr Douglas?' Elinor couldn't for the life of her bring him to mind. Or Miss Holloway, either. 'Oh, well,' she murmured. 'I won't be there after all. Why should I care?'

Mrs Hatcher waited for a while, then in the absence of any other comment from Elinor, she said, 'So that's agreed, then? Mr Douglas and Miss Holloway.'

Elinor waved a limp hand. 'Whatever, dear. I really can't be bothered.'

It was quite clear that Elinor was tiring fast. Not only that, but someone was coming up the path. Mrs Hatcher waited for the doorbell to ring, but clearly the newcomer carried her own key for, after letting herself in, she went straight to the kitchen. No doubt whoever it was would interrupt them soon enough, so Esme Hatcher hurried on. 'So this, the extra, is going to go to—' She glanced at the old will. 'Megan Elizabeth, or Victoria Ann?'

The strange effect of seeing things through streaks of glistening ice had suddenly come back to distract Elinor. Oh, God! Another horror! Was she going blind?

'Tory,' she said, forgetting how the question had been put to her – about money received or money owed. 'Victoria Ann.'

She sounded definite, so Esme made one last quick note.

*

As she was coming through her mother's front gate next morning, Megan saw one of the carers heading for the wheelie bin, stored at the side of the house. She hurried over, glad to get the chance of a quick word. She held the lid up while the carer dropped two tightly knotted plastic bags into the bin, then asked, 'So how's it going? How's my Mum today?'

The carer pushed back straggling hair. 'Not much change. Still a bit confused.' She glanced towards the house as if to check that Elinor wasn't watching through a window. 'Actually, there is something. I wouldn't want to talk of it in front of your mother. She would be mortified. But these pads that the district nurses keep on sending her—'

'Pads?'

'You know. For the incontinence.'

Megan was shocked. 'No. No, I didn't know!'

'Well, to be fair, it's only been the last few days that Elinor's had to use them all the time. But they are not the nicest.'

'No,' Megan said. 'I can imagine. Not the nicest thing at all!'

The carer said, 'No, dear. What I meant is they're not the nicest sort that you can get. They chafe. I think that they're too wide and thick, and quite a lot of my old ladies have a problem with them.'

'Oh.'

'Well, what it boils down to is that Elinor isn't as comfortable as she might be. So I was wondering if you or your sister wouldn't mind—'

'Getting the right sort? No, not at all. I'll go right now, if you can tell me what I should be buying.'

'The trouble is that Elinor really doesn't want you and your sister to know she's reached this state. She's horribly embarrassed. And I wouldn't be surprised if she's also worried that you might get upset.'

Megan was close to tears. 'Poor thing. Well, could I maybe sneak them in and hide them somewhere? Then you can all pretend these are a new sort she's been sent, and she won't know I know.'

'That cupboard under the stairs? We're keeping quite a lot of stuff in there right now.'

'Of course! And if they've got the right kind in that pharmacy at Kingsford Corner, I can be back in twenty minutes or so.'

She couldn't wait to get away and do something useful for her mother. Something kind. Incontinence! She knew her mother well enough to know that nothing – nothing in the world – could humiliate her more. Was that what had been in those plastic bags? Sodden wet pads, dealt with by someone who was practically a stranger? Oh, cancer was dreadful! Dreadful! No one should have to suffer such indignities, and for someone like Elinor it must be truly awful.

She'd almost rushed away before the carer could tell her which brand to buy. And even as she reached the gate, she was called back again. 'Megan, if it takes longer than you think, I might be gone. So sneak a couple onto the pile in that small cabinet beside the downstairs loo, and when I'm back this afternoon, I'll say I left them there. Oh, and be warned, your mother might have someone with her.'

'The nurse?'

'No, a solicitor.'

'Really?'

'Yes. She came yesterday, and told your mother she'd be back some time this morning for a signature.' The carer sighed. 'I'd hoped to get your mother upstairs for a little rest. She's really quite washed out. But there you go.'

'Yes,' Megan said. Her head was spinning. She felt overwhelmed with some new feeling. Confidence, was it? Sudden assurance? Her mother was about to put things right! She must be loved. She must.

She slid back in her car and pulled out from the kerb, not even noticing the car that had drawn up behind, waiting to take her place.

*

All the way to the pharmacy, Megan was in turmoil. How could she ever have doubted that blood was, after all, thicker than water? All of these years she'd felt on the edge of things, as if her mother's sympathies had somehow lain much more with Tory than with her.

But now she knew that she'd been wrong. Gordon might have written all those cheques for Tory, but everyone knew Elinor left everything to do with finance up to him. For one thing, it was his money, not hers. And for another, Elinor had been brought up to think it was a bit indelicate for women to be good with invoices and interest rates and things like that. How startled she had been to learn that both her daughters had their own bank accounts! In her old-fashioned marriage, Gordon took care of everything. From Elinor's point of view the money simply floated in and floated out. She could write cheques, of course, and had a bank card which she rarely used. 'I'm running short,' she used to say despairingly as she peered in her purse. And Gordon would flip a few notes off the wad he kept in his breast pocket. 'There you are, Duchess! That'll keep you going.'

Maybe she'd truly never realised just how much was going Tory's way. It's not as if anyone made any fuss. The topic never arose. Why should it? Till Megan idly flicked through the cheque stubs while she was picking out the paperwork for the solicitor, nobody knew.

Except for Tory and Barry. But to be fair they'd never tried to hide the fact that they'd had all that extra loot. It simply hadn't come up. And that was understandable. The sheer discrepancy between the financial states of the two families was so enormous that no one ever raised the topic. She and her sister were no longer close enough to leap that psychic barrier. Megan and Malcolm almost seemed to make a point of never mentioning anything like a rise in school fees, or the price of their new cars. And Tory and Barry stolidly affected indifference to any sudden dips in their own standard of living.

No one had ever lied. And, for all Megan knew, Tory and Barry hadn't even disingenuously kept their own counsel. They more than likely had assumed that handouts had been doled out fairly equally to both the families. After all, Tory had been startled enough back in Ben's Bistro when Megan raised the issue of the legacies within the will – even implied that Megan was being petty. She wouldn't ever have dared to take that line if she had known she'd done much better all along.

And now it seems her mother, freed at last from Gordon's baleful influence, had called in a solicitor to change the will. She'd risen above her pain and the humiliations of incontinence to put things right. And just in time. If Gordon had had his way, the horrid business would never have been sorted.

Gordon. Bloody Gordon. In his own quiet way he'd been a troublemaker from the start, making things harder for Megan. If he'd not muscled in on Elinor so soon after their father's death – moved in and taken over – then Megan might have had a chance to grieve more openly. She might have come to terms. If she'd not been so tangled up in her resentments of this man who took her father's place, but wasn't him, she would, she was quite sure, have managed to be happier.

More like her sister. Easy-going, even.

He was the root of all the trouble, Gordon. And he had hated her. That is what Malcolm said – that he had hated her. All of those years. And he'd been so unfair. Look at that quite amazing business of Tory and Barry's sneakily offensive wedding. He had forgiven her. He'd started off quite as disgusted with the pair of them as everyone else had been. She could remember what he said when they came back, so smugly, with their Big News. 'Slunk off to get married without a word to anyone? Who do you think you are? Romeo and Juliet? Or the first mixed-race couple in some redneck state? How could you have humiliated Elinor this way? What has she ever done to make you think that, if you'd said you would prefer a quiet wedding, just the two of you, she wouldn't have accepted it? But not to say a word! To sneak away and leave her to explain to friends and neighbours that she didn't even know – that her own daughter has treated her with such contempt!' He'd turned to Barry. 'Out of this house, right now! The very sight of you repels me!'

Tory had scuttled out after her new husband. And three months later the offence was pretty well forgotten! If Megan herself had ever behaved like that, she never would have been forgiven, let alone bankrolled through years and years of semi-idleness and feckless living.

Bloody Gordon! Bloody, bloody Gordon! Thank God the man was dead and Elinor was free to be herself again.

A proper mother.

Megan pulled up in the small car park opposite the pharmacy and for a minute or two she didn't move. She felt as if her heart were softening inside her breast. Literally softening. She hadn't realised it for such a long while, but she still loved her family. They still loved her, that was quite obvious. And she loved them.

*

Elinor saw Megan's distinctive silver saloon car drawing away and wondered why her daughter hadn't come inside the house, even for a moment. Had she gone back for something she'd forgotten? Perhaps there'd been a sudden call from one of her girls. (That was the nice thing about Tory's visits. Nobody interrupted them. No mobile ever rang to distract Tory or summon her home. She didn't even seem to keep a phone inside her pocket or her bag. Or, if she did, she never switched it on.)

Then Elinor saw a woman coming up the path. Oh, not another new face! You'd think the Home Care Service could pay employees well enough to keep them in the job. She'd seen this one before though, she was sure. And finally it came to her that this was Mrs Hatcher, who'd visited the previous day. My! She'd been quick off the mark. Perhaps Russell Powers Solicitors were worrying that if they didn't get their skates on and their invoice in, they'd be too late to be paid.

Don't think that way!

Elinor made an effort to be welcoming. 'You are an angel, saving me the effort of coming to your office.'

'All part of the service.'

'Would you like tea?'

Mrs Hatcher had appointments from half past twelve, so shook her head. 'It's just a flying visit. The will's redone. All I need now is to read through to check we have it right, then you can sign it.'

'I'm sure you've got it just the way I want it.'

'I certainly hope I have. But it's important to be sure.'

So Elinor leaned back as Esme Hatcher droned her way through the provisions of the will. She wasn't comfortable. And she was anxious suddenly that there might be a leakage. What was that sickly smell? Please God, it wasn't what she feared. She must have put the damn thing on right, but they were so bulky they rucked up. Was that enough to make the sides leak? Oh, this was misery! The sooner it was over, the better.

'Dear, would you do me a favour? Pour me a little water from that jug?'

Esme jumped to her feet. 'I'll get some fresh.'

While Mrs Hatcher ran the tap in the kitchen, Elinor slid another painkiller into her mouth. No doubt the carers would notice. But she could argue that she'd knocked the dosette box onto the floor, and any pills they thought were missing must have rolled under the sofa. She sipped the water Esme brought to her, and then leaned back, thinking again about the way that Megan had arrived but instantly rushed off. It was a mystery.

Finally Esme reached the end of her brief exposition of the will's main points. 'So that's what you'll be signing. Are you completely sure you're happy with it? You can still change your mind.'

'Change my mind?'

'You know.' Mrs Hatcher rose. 'About leaving so much more money to Victoria than to Megan.'

She'd got the two of them the wrong way round, Elinor noted. But what did that matter so long as it was down the right way in the will. 'Is that it? Should I sign?'

'We'll need a witness, of course.'

Elinor panicked. Oh, God! She wasn't going to go next door and ask Anne Taylor in. She was quite sure that weird, sweet smell was getting stronger. And the damn woman would be bound to take the opportunity to hang around and witter on about that crumbling wall. 'Really? You couldn't witness it yourself?'

'No, no. That's unprofessional, I'm afraid. I thought perhaps whoever it is who's just started vacuuming upstairs?'

Of course! Mrs Deloy. She came when she was called, and though she seemed unusually anxious about this added duty – not to say downright unwilling – Mrs Hatcher soon prevailed and, within moments, Elinor's will was done.

Part 2

9.

Tory was sitting on the faded old pouffe, trying to cut the claggy patches out of Archie's rarely-brushed coat. Each time she got her nail scissors round one of the lumps, the dog lurched even more strongly in his efforts to get away.

'Want me to hold him?' offered Barry.

'I'm very cross at having to do this at all,' said Tory. 'I paid for all those batteries for Ned's new whatsit, and in return he was to get this job done for me by this weekend.'

'Why? Is something happening?'

Tory looked up. 'You know that something's happening. This afternoon Megan is dropping off those chairs we chose from Mum's house.'

'I thought we would be fetching them ourselves.'

'We were. But then Megan thought she'd rather like to take that weird old dresser from Mum's guest bedroom. For that she needed one of their work vans, and so she offered to bung in our stuff and drop it off here today.'

'I see.' He clamped his knees on either side of Archie, who panicked and yelped. Barry said, 'Shut up, Archie. You're just a giant baby. Nobody's hurting you,' then added to his wife, 'So why's it so important that Archie's tidied up?'

Tory kept snipping. 'Because, last time Megan came, she spent the whole time doing this job herself, and I felt terrible. She said that, if you leave the claggy bits for too long, dogs can get maggots.'

'Maggots? Oh, that's disgusting.'

'And I was going to clean out the fridge.'

He tried to look on the bright side. 'Maybe she won't come in. Maybe she'll wait till we've unloaded all our stuff, and then drive off.'

'Fat chance,' said Tory. 'Haven't you noticed that ever since Mum went into St Bride's and we've been closing down the house, Megan has never missed a chance for a sisterly chat.'

'I did think she was easier. I never put it down to Elinor moving into the hospice.'

'It isn't that. It's talking about Gordon. She wants to do it all the time now. She's become obsessed. "Do you remember when Gordon did this?" And, "Am I right in thinking that Gordon once said the other?" It's as if Megan's set herself some sort of test – trying to reconstruct every last thing Gordon said or did from the first day Mum met him.'

'I didn't think she even liked him much.'

'She didn't.'

Then the scissors slipped and Archie yelped again. 'Oh, bugger it!' Tory pushed Barry's knees apart so Archie could escape. 'We'll just have to shut him in a bedroom.'

'Shall I start on the fridge?'

'Too late. I'll have to make sure everything we need for tea is out, all ready on a tray.'

'What a performance.'

'I wouldn't mind,' said Tory. 'Except that Gordon is dead. So what on earth's the bloody point?'

'Perhaps she's feeling guilty about how she treated him.'

'That's not the feeling I get. Not at all.'

He shrugged. 'Well, maybe it's just something she can talk about with Elinor. You've said yourself how very tiring it can be, thinking of things to say.'

'That might have been the case a couple of weeks ago. But there's no talking to Mum now. She's pretty well out of it. I bet that Megan simply does what I do – sits holding Mum's hand and chatting away about all sorts of nonsense while she watches the clock.'

'You must have some idea what's going on. She is your sister.'

But Tory couldn't put her finger on it. So she let it go, and kept to worrying about the state of the dog and the fridge.

*

Megan was all too quick to say yes to a cup of tea, and take a seat at the table. Tory put down the tray. 'Biscuit?'

'No, thanks.'

Ned turned from something he was gluing messily beside the kettle and reached an arm across Megan. 'I'll have one.'

It took a bit of self-control on Megan's part not to say something sharp to him about his manners. But she had bigger fish to fry. 'Tory, do you remember when we went to Stanton Beach?'

'Stanton Beach?'

'You know. Near Great Aunt Elspeth's house. That place where we hired bikes. You had to be on a tandem with Gordon because you weren't quite steady enough to ride your own two-wheeler without wobbling.'

Without thinking, Tory brushed all her biscuit crumbs off the table onto the floor. 'I do remember the tandem.'

'Do you remember getting an ice cream afterwards?'

'No.'

'Really? It was a strawberry one.'

Tory began to feel uneasy. 'Well, what about it? We must have slurped up countless ice creams in our time, especially at beaches. What was so special about these?'

'Well, that's the point, really. It wasn't these. It was just yours.'

'Sorry?'

Megan leaned over the table. 'I didn't get one. We cycled for ages and ages, and it was awfully warm. You probably don't remember because Gordon did the pedalling on yours. But I was as hot as anything by the time Mum spotted that ice cream seller on his weird bike thing, and waved him down.

'I don't remember that.'

But Megan was unstoppable. 'So we all leaned the bikes against the boardwalk railings. Mum started rooting in her purse and Gordon said, 'Oh, don't be silly, Elinor,' and whipped out that shiny leather wallet, the way he always did, and strode across the road towards the ice cream bloke.'

'How can you remember all this?'

'And he was there for quite a while, and then he came back carrying three ices. Three!'

'Maybe Mum didn't want—'

'No! You're not getting it! They were all strawberry. And he gave one to Mum and one to you, and said to me, "I'm really sorry, Megan, but strawberry's the only flavour he has, and you don't like that so I didn't get you one."'

116

Tory was baffled. 'Did you like strawberry?' Then she remembered. 'No, you didn't, did you?'

'No. I hated strawberry and I still do.'

'So what's your point?'

'My point,' said Megan, 'is that I can't believe that ice cream seller only sold one flavour.'

Now Tory stared. 'You're telling me you think that Gordon was lying?'

'Don't you?'

For just a moment, Tory couldn't think of what to say.

Megan persisted, 'Ask yourself, is it likely? A summer's day. A chest of ices on the front of this bloke's bike, and only strawberry? If he was going to sell only one flavour, it would have been vanilla.'

'Perhaps strawberry was the only flavour he had left. You said yourself that it was a hot day.'

'No,' Megan told her firmly. 'I think it was an act of petty spite.'

She raised her mug for the first time to sip her tea while Tory sat in silence, noticing that even Ned, who generally took an interest only in himself, was standing stock-still, staring at his aunt.

*

Megan was on her knees outside the front door, brushing dried mud off the boot scraper. 'I don't think she believed me,' she said to Malcolm. 'I think she thought I was imagining it.' She sighed. 'This must be what it's like to be in one of those families where half the children think they had a happy childhood, and half of them don't. Everyone sees things differently and none of the interpretations match. I'm just surprised that she was so surprised. Because you really would have thought that Tory would have noticed she was the favoured one. She must have known that she was spoiled rotten by the man.'

He'd realised over the last weeks that it was best to tread carefully. 'I expect she did. But to be fair, knowing her stepfather found her a whole lot easier than he found you doesn't mean Tory would automatically assume the worst about a missing ice cream.'

'I suppose not. I mean, if you yourself have no reason to think the man was taking some sort of sneaky revenge at every opportunity he had...'

'But even you can't be sure...'

'Oh, I'm sure.'

Malcolm didn't push his luck. He knew that she was in a state, and put it down to all the gathering anguish about her mother. And things were ghastly there, for Elinor had turned into a skeleton with yellow skin. Last time he went into the hospice room to fetch his wife, he truly thought he'd found her talking to a corpse.

Best to lighten things up a bit. 'Let's give a thought to lunch. Perhaps you'd like to go out for a change?'

'I'll get this finished.'

'Megan, it's a boot scraper! It's supposed to be dirty.'

He tried to tug her to her feet, but she resisted him. He felt quite awful. This was all his doing. He'd wriggled out of having to confess to one small sin by blackening Gordon's name. But his suggestion that her stepfather had hated her had instantly grown wings and taken off. There was no telling where this business would end. Each night he lay in bed listening to his wife's fast-lengthening litany of disinterred resentments against Gordon, thinking, 'This is my fault. I must tell Megan the truth.' He'd plan to come clean first thing in the morning. Then, over his first coffee, he'd baulk at the idea, assuring himself that, though the details of these ancient grudges were probably imagined, at heart the accusation was spot on. Gordon had been most unfair. So why should he, Malcolm, take the rap when Gordon had more than earned his reputation for inequity – and also had the singular advantage of being buried, and unable to defend himself.

And so the days went by. At breakfast time she'd suddenly remember Gordon calling her 'Clever-clogs'. 'That wasn't very nice.'

He'd come as close as he dare to speaking up for the dead man he'd so deliberately maligned. 'Maybe you'd won some prize. He may have meant it as a compliment.'

'Oh, I don't think so!'

An hour later, searching for one of the stiff brushes they used to clean the printer heads, she'd start to talk about the time Gordon had snapped at her for using his shaving brush to paint a sky blue wash background over a sheet of paper. 'It was a water-based paint, for heaven's sake! If Tory had done that, I don't think he'd have said a word – not even ordered her to rinse the brush out properly. He'd just have laughed, and praised her for being so inventive.'

'Well, she was younger, I suppose...'

As they undressed at night, he'd try to steer her onto other topics. 'I thought we might start thinking about a short break, once we're free. I know you won't want to be away while Elinor's in St Bride's. But maybe afterwards—'

All roads, it seemed, led back to Rome. 'Gordon took us to Shropshire once. Did you know that? It was pure nastiness. I'd just made all my choices for the sixth form, and opted for Classics. So I was longing – absolutely longing – to go to Italy or Greece. And we had always gone abroad in summer. Gordon would claim he needed sun and didn't give a toss which country he was in so long as it was warm. And just because, that year, I really, really wanted to walk round ruins and get a head start, he stubbornly insisted we went to Shropshire. Sodden wet Shropshire! Jesus!'

In the end, naturally, Malcolm gave up.

*

The hospice made the call at half past nine at night. Tory was in the middle of ticking Lindy off about some lies she'd told – 'How are we ever supposed to trust you?' – when Barry tapped her on the shoulder and passed her the phone. 'You have to take this. It's St Bride's.'

His tone of voice was serious enough for Lindy to deduce the row was over. But out of curiosity, she stayed.

'Yes... Yes... Yes, I would... Yes... Yes... I'll phone my sister. Yes, I'll do that now. We'll probably both come in.'

'Is Granny dying?' Lindy asked.

'Yes.' Tory punched out her sister's number. 'Malcolm? Sorry to bother you. Can I have Megan? The hospice just rang. It's about Mum.'

He didn't hold her up with pleasantries. He simply gave the phone to Megan. Tory explained. 'The hospice say that, if we want to be there, we should come in now. So shall I meet you there?'

Barry's hand dropped on her shoulder. 'Tell her you've drunk too much to drive.'

Tory was startled. 'Have I?'

'You definitely have. Ask Megan if she'll pick you up.'

Tory said into the phone, 'Did you hear that? Barry says I can't drive, so will you pick me up?'

It was arranged. The sisters sat together as the warm and comfortable car purred down the quiet roads towards St Bride's. 'I could sit here for

119

ever,' Tory told her sister. 'It's bliss, this car. And once we prise ourselves out of it, it's going to be a horrid, horrid night, then weeks of arrangements. I can't bear the thought.'

'It won't be nearly as bad as Gordon's service,' Megan assured her, 'because we won't have Mum's feelings to worry about, the way we did back then.'

'I suppose you're right.' Tory peered out into the velvet night, stroked by occasional headlights. 'And I expect Gordon had Mum's funeral sorted out as well.'

'Bits of it.'

'Action replay?'

'Not really, no,' said Megan. 'This will be different. It will be in church.'

'In church? Not in the crematorium, like Gordon's?'

'No.'

'Really?'

'Mum doesn't want a crematorium job,' said Megan. 'She's changed her mind and has decided to be buried.'

Tory glanced at her sister. 'News to me. Did she tell someone at St Bride's?'

'No, she told me.'

'When?'

'Several times. It was important to her, I could tell.'

'That's very strange. She never said a word to me.' Tory shrugged. 'Though, to be fair, I haven't thought that she's made sense at all since she's been in there. We haven't managed any real conversations. I burble on, but I get nothing back. How come she's managed to get through to you?'

'I don't know, but she did. And she was adamant.'

'That's very odd.'

The sisters sat in silence for a while, then Tory said, 'Where will the service be, then? Mum hasn't been in any church as long as I can remember.'

'She's been in ours,' Megan said stiffly. 'For both girls' christenings and Amy's confirmation.'

'Oh, right,' said Tory, and she blushed, remembering that she and Barry had turned down invitations to attend. 'Sorry about that.'

'We'll have the service at our Saint Edmund's, then the interment can be a private family matter.'

'Why? Won't some of her friends want to come? Neighbours and carers? Mrs Deloy? I think they'd like to be there for the whole caboodle.'

'It's a long way to go.'

'The graveyard? Isn't it beside the church?'

'But Mum's not going to be buried there. Her grave's to be in Childon, with our dad.'

Reaching the hospice gates she slowed the car, remembering the speed bumps, and in the dark she didn't see the look of sheer astonishment on Tory's face.

10.

Malcolm went upstairs at midnight. There'd been no news. For days now Megan had been telling him that Elinor could not communicate. But he still worried. People did rally on deathbeds. He'd heard of that, or maybe read about it in old books. He could imagine Elinor suddenly snapping open her eyes and fixing Megan with a glittering stare. 'You know how much Gordon loved you. So don't believe a word of it if anyone tells you otherwise.'

Stop it! Ridiculous! He hadn't tried to talk to Elinor himself, but he had heard enough from Megan to know that she was drugged way beyond making sense. The most the woman could do was feebly squeeze her daughter's hand and mumble incoherently. No one had understood a word she'd said for two weeks now. There was no possibility that he'd be rumbled. Sometime in the next hours there'd be a text from Megan saying Elinor was dead. The danger would be over. He would be home and dry, his hateful, stupid little lie mercifully concealed for ever.

He checked his phone was on. He took a shower. He tried to read the paper. Five to one. He slid across to Megan's side of the bed, which the electric blanket had been warming for the last hour, and read four pages of his book. He rose to open the curtains and stare at the scudding moon. (So beautiful and so extraordinary. Ought to do that more often.)

And then, at ten to two, he heard the little ping.

There was the message: *All over. xxxx*

Thank God for that! All over! And, from the kisses, it was obvious that Megan didn't mean their marriage, or her trust in him. There was no longer any chance of being held to account. He'd gambled, and he'd won. He'd never make the same mistake again. He couldn't even think why he had ever for a moment thought it might be worth dabbling in such dishonesty for such a petty sum. He must have been an idiot. Money was earned honestly so much more easily.

Now he could sleep. He wouldn't ever have to wake again, deep in the night, with that sick, anxious feeling. The risk was gone. All over. Malcolm tugged at the pillow till it was bunched under his chin, slid his hands down between his thighs for idle comfort, and fell so deeply asleep that even Megan's homecoming an hour later failed to wake him. She had to push him very hard indeed to make a space on hers, the warmer side.

*

Barry watched football. Part of him thought he ought to stay dressed and downstairs, in case he had to nip out to St Bride's to fetch Tory home. With luck, Megan would drop her off just as she'd picked her up. But Tory claimed that Megan had been grimly assiduous in all her hospice visits over the last couple of weeks, sitting at Elinor's bedside hour after hour. She'd more than once suggested that her sister might crumple totally when the moment came.

That would presumably make Megan unfit to drive. But, on the other hand, by now Tory would be stone sober. Would she be allowed to take the wheel?

Probably not. Bloody expensive car, that thing of Megan's. Hugely powerful. Barry would bet that the insurance covered named drivers only. Better stay dressed, in case.

But, hell. It might be hours and hours. Or days. Nobody really knew when somebody was going to croak. He could just go upstairs, take off his shoes and have a nap on the bed. Yes, he'd do that. He'd be less tired in the morning, but still on call to shoot off to St Bride's should it be necessary.

Or they could get a taxi. Megan could afford it. Barry's warm, striped pyjamas were calling to him from beneath the pillows. And how long would it take to dress again if he were needed? Two minutes? Three at the most. It's not as if he were a woman, after all, with all that fastening and pulling straight. He could be ready in no time.

Barry crawled into bed and dutifully stared at his mobile. He could leave it on all night, but that would risk Tory waking him out of pure boredom, borrowing Megan's phone to text some quite unnecessary update – *Won't be long now* – or some such.

No. Switch the bloody thing off, as usual. Tory could always ring the landline if she needed him. It mostly worked now, after that last young engineer's visit. That way Tory would know she would risk waking everyone, so she would only bother if it was important.

Yes. That was the best plan by far.

Barry rolled over and fell fast asleep.

*

'How do you feel?' asked Tory.

Megan made a face. 'I don't know. How do you?'

'I don't know, either. It feels odd. Not totally real.'

'I suppose we've known for so long now that it was coming.'

'Odd, though,' said Tory, 'that it was so easy to tell.'

'The exact moment? Yes, I thought that. I mean, it wasn't really anything at all to do with breathing, was it? It was just something about the face.'

'You can see why they used to think the spirit left the body.'

'Well, in a way it does.'

'I suppose so.'

They sat in silence for a while. The night nurse put her head around the door to offer them another pot of tea. 'What do you think?' asked Tory.

'I think, to be honest, I'd quite like to go home.'

'Me, too.'

Megan turned back to the nurse. 'Would that be all right? If we just went home, and came back in the morning?'

The answer was as they expected. Tory went off to the loo while Megan gathered up their bags, and one or two of Elinor's things. 'I'll leave the rest till tomorrow.'

The moon raced overhead. 'Fabulous night,' said Tory. 'You think of death for someone as ill as Elinor was at the end as being sort of not all that important. Just the inevitable end. And given how far down she'd gone, a total relief. And then you see a moon like this and think that being alive is everything. Everything!'

The car lights blinked, and they climbed in. 'I feel quite weird,' said Tory. 'As if we're miles away from real life. On the moon.'

'That's the good thing about this car,' said Megan. 'It runs so smoothly that it's hard to believe that what you're seeing through the windscreen is actually real. Especially at night.'

Tory said nothing, but she thought her sister very odd. She had expected tears, hysteria, whole tempests of emotion. Megan had spent so many hours at their mother's bedside in the last two weeks. Yet here she was, as calm as anything, mistaking Tory's strange and wistful mood for some remark about the car.

'What will we do?' she asked a minute or so later. 'Should we arrange to meet there in the morning and divvy up the things that have to be done?'

'Not there,' said Megan. 'They'll have moved Mum out of her room by then. She'll be at Harper's.'

'Really? So shall we meet there? At the funeral home?'

'I can sort all that out, if you'd prefer.'

'You're sounding very calm. Are you sure you're all right?'

Megan glanced over. 'You don't think I'm trying to take over?'

Tory did, really. But she wasn't in the slightest sorry. One funeral in the year was quite enough. 'No, not at all. It's just that you're the one with a real job. And this stuff chews up so much time. Decisions. Flowers. Music. Announcements. Cars. Solicitors. And all those bloody forms.'

But Megan was already turning into Staines Crescent. What a swift ride. All of the lights had been green. And Tory was exhausted. She'd be quite mad to stay inside the car and argue for the right to do the sort of stuff she hated doing. If Megan chose to take control of the whole lot, then good for her.

Tory reached for her bag and slid out of the car. 'Listen,' she said. 'We can do anything you ask us. Anything. Just say the word, and Barry and I will jump to it. That's a promise.'

She leaned across and kissed her sister on the cheek. 'Goodnight!'

'Goodnight.'

Even before Tory had slid her front door key into the lock, Megan had sped away.

*

Barry was astonished. 'She's to be buried at Childon? With your dad?'

'That is what Megan said.'

Ned, who was eavesdropping, broke in with some amazement of his own. 'In the same coffin? With the rotted body?'

'Don't be so daft,' said Tory. 'Just in the same plot. And her name will be added to the gravestone.'

'Creepy!' said Lou.

'Sick!' Lindy muttered.

Barry ignored his children. 'What about Gordon?'

Tory shrugged. 'I don't know. I don't know anything about these things. I can't believe it's normal to be put in with your first husband if your second husband has a plot of his own.'

'Or is alive,' said Lindy.

'Or is alive,' agreed Tory. 'But Megan says that Mum chose burial, and Gordon isn't anywhere, is he?'

Now Barry raised an eyebrow at his wife. 'Oh, no?'

'Oh, Christ!' said Tory. 'He's not still in the cupboard under the stairs?'

'I think you'll find he is.'

He'd barely finished saying it before the children got there. 'Come out!' shrieked Tory. 'Don't you dare!' But they were far too old to be bossed around that easily. Ned came out carrying the box. Lou shrieked, pretending she was horrified, and Lindy curled her lip. 'That is disgusting! Our coats are in there! That's just horrible.'

Ned plonked the box on the table as Tory pushed Archie's questing nose away. 'Can we see what's inside?'

'No, you cannot!'

'Oh, go on!'

'No!'

'I've never seen Fried Grandpa.'

He'd gone too far. He was manhandled from the room by Barry, and once it was clear that no one was going to open up the box, Lindy and Lou drifted off.

'Oh, God!' said Tory. 'How could I possibly have forgotten?'

'You have had other things on your mind.'

'I know. But, really! Gordon's ashes in the cupboard! All this time!'

'It hasn't been that long.'

'Long enough.' She pushed the box a little further away. 'What do we do with them now?'

'The kids?'

'No.' Tory read the label. '"The cremated remains of Gordon James Forsyth." Can't he be taken somewhere?'

'What, dumped?'

'No, not exactly. But, now Mum's dead, couldn't he just be scattered in some field, or something?'

'Not very ecologically sound.'

'A river?'

'Probably worse.'

'Oh, God! Well, what do people do with sodding ashes when they're stuck with them?'

'Megan will know.'

'Of course. Megan will know.'

'The most important thing right now is to tuck them away somewhere that Ned can't find them.'

'Fat chance in this house.'

He looked at the clock. Eight thirty. Kick-off time. He had been looking forward to the match all day. 'Why don't we lock them in the boot of the car, and think of somewhere sensible tomorrow?'

So that's what they did.

*

Tory did charge her phone, but Megan didn't ring all morning. In the end, Tory got bored and said to Barry, 'I might nip off to yoga.'

'Yoga?'

'You promise you won't tell? If Megan gets you on the phone, you'll tell her that I'm laying in some groceries or something.' He hadn't looked at her accusingly but still she felt obliged to offer a defence. 'It's just that Megan's taken charge and I've got nothing to do. I'm flapping round the house to no real purpose.'

'You do whatever you like. It must have been a grim two weeks. I'll provide cover if your sister phones to ask why you're not present at the Washing of the Corpse.' Catching his wife's little shudder, he turned the joke by adding hastily, 'Or at the Reading of the Will.'

'The Reading of the Will doesn't take place, except in films and novels.'

'Doesn't it?'

'No. Well, that's what Megan says, and she seems to have turned herself into the world's greatest expert on matters funerary, and everything to do with inheritance.'

'Good thing your mother changed her will, then. Or Megan might have flounced off, leaving it all to you, and you'd have missed your yoga.' He added as an afterthought, 'Elinor did change it, didn't she?'

'Oh, yes. She changed it. Mrs Deloy told Megan she was called down from vacuuming to be a witness. She seemed quite worried about it,

Megan said, and needed quite a lot of reassurance that she'd done the right thing.' Tory sighed. 'God knows how much extra Mum decided to shove Megan's way. And God knows whether Megan will reckon it's enough.' Tory picked up her bag. 'I'm off. Ned should be back at half past three.'

'I have to be at work well before then. I think they're waiting for me to be late again, so they can pounce.'

'Oh, dear.' Tory put down her bag. 'I'd better stay then.' Barely a moment passed before she picked it up again, 'Oh, bugger it! Ned knows the key is in the shed, and he'll be fine for half an hour on his own.'

'You bet. He'll spend the whole time searching for his grandpa's ashes.'

Both of them burst out laughing. 'Are they still in the car? I must ask Megan what to do with them.'

And out she went.

*

Lou came home from school to find Ned hauling things out of his parents' bedroom cupboard and stacking them behind him. 'What are you doing?'

'Looking for Grandpa's ashes.'

'Why?'

'I want to see what they look like.'

'They'll look like ashes, I suppose.'

'They won't. I went online and it says that they're hard and weird and heavier than you think. And sort of crusty.'

'Ee-ew! Where's Mum?'

'I reckon she's at yoga. Her mat's gone.'

'You'll catch it if she finds you messing in her cupboard.'

'I do this all the time,' he said. 'It's where she hides our presents and our Easter eggs, and she's never caught me yet.'

Lou dropped on her knees beside him. 'So is it there, that box?'

'No.' Ned began pushing everything around him back into the cupboard. 'What do they do with ashes anyway?'

'They sprinkle them,' said Lou. 'And sometimes, if two people are in love and die together, then they mingle them.'

'How do you know that?'

'Everyone knows that.'

'What, just stir both lots up, then sprinkle them together? They can't be planning to do that because Mum said that Granny's being buried.'

'Maybe they'll throw the ashes in the grave.'

Ned's eyes gleamed. 'What, unscrew the coffin lid and pour them in? So I might get to see my first dead body!'

'Don't be ridiculous,' said Lou. 'They'd never in a million years do that. It's probably illegal. No, they'll just scatter them on top.'

Her sheer contempt had ended their unusual patch of intimacy. Ned slid the last few things back in the cupboard and waited till he heard his sister shut her bedroom door before he followed her out of the room.

*

At first Megan was startled. 'Elinor changed her executors? What, dropped us both, me and Victoria?'

Though there was no need, Kevin Douglas made the gesture of glancing down as if to check. 'That's right. In this new will your mother asked Mrs Hatcher to appoint myself and one of the firm's other partners.'

Megan said thoughtfully, 'I wonder why she did that.' And then it came to her. It was to make things easier. After all, Elinor had just been changing her will in Megan's favour. Admittedly, that was at Tory's request (technically speaking). But still it might have been a little awkward, especially if her sister later formed regrets about her generous, easy-going attitude. So Elinor had shown real sensitivity in making that change too, along with the provisions of the will. Of course, it might have been Mrs Hatcher who suggested it. But Elinor had obviously been trying hard to make amends for Gordon's spite. This would have been just one more thoughtful gesture towards the daughter Gordon had been treating so unfairly over past years.

Mr Douglas, to his astonishment, saw her face soften. Had she not realised quite how drastically her mother had re-jigged the will? He hoped she wouldn't suddenly demand to know the details. But rather as if she was interpreting her mother's change of executors as a hint that she shouldn't press him further on the matter, she just said pleasantly enough, 'So my sister and I no longer have to do anything? We just get on with sorting out the funeral, and leave the rest to you?'

He nodded. 'That's about it. I hope it won't take long. There are a few loose ends in your stepfather's estate. But once they're tidied away and everything has been subsumed into your late mother's affairs, we can get cracking.'

'No hurry,' she said almost automatically, and smiled again.

The longer that he sat and watched, the more he thought she didn't realise what was going on and what was going to hit her. Tempted to probe, he leaned a little closer over the desk and asked her casually, 'So you would not, right now, envisage any problems?'

'Problems?'

He came quite close to brutally posing the question. He could explain the changes and ask if she'd be formulating any plan to contest this new will. Her mother, after all, had been so ill. Cancer could go to the brain and make the sanest person do the oddest things. But then he realised he had another meeting on the hour, and not quite enough time to look through the papers again. If Mrs Forsyth's daughter was going to raise a stink, she could come back another time or pay her own solicitor. He had just slid this visit in between appointments as a courtesy, and he was not inclined to let his schedule slip on her account.

As once before, he showed the interview was over by getting to his feet and handing over the expensive coat he'd hung up earlier. 'Regretfully...'

She smiled a third time and it struck him suddenly: not only did she fail to appreciate what had happened, but she was in this better mood because she thought her mother had called Mrs Hatcher in to rectify the small anomaly that had been bugging her the last time that they met – that legacy for the third child.

Dear gods, he truly wouldn't want to be around when she found out.

She shook his hand and thanked him for his time. He closed the door behind her, then opened it again to watch her down the stairs.

Could it be possible that this new partner, who had come with such cast-iron references, had got the new will all wrong?

No, not that. It was such an awful thought, he couldn't entertain it.

11.

Megan decided it would be a rush to hold the funeral and the interment on the same day. 'So what we're going to do is hold the service in the church. The funeral directors will drive the coffin down to Childon overnight, and we'll have the interment next morning.'

Tory agreed. (She didn't have much option. All the arrangements had been made.) The children moaned a bit. 'Oh, not two things! Can't I just come to one?', 'What time will we be back? I'm definitely not going to miss Ali's party!', 'Why do we have to come? She won't be there when we get buried.'

But Tory hadn't yet forgotten their behaviour last time. She gave all three of them the ticking off of their lives. She threatened them with no allowance – no, not for months – if they let her down again. She ordered them to wear their darkest and most sober clothes. And she warned Lou that if she so much as sniffed once, let alone sobbed aloud, she'd never get to go shopping in town with her friends again, let alone to any parties. No, never again!

They didn't for a moment believe her threats, but this clear proof of how much they had shamed her last time chastened all of them. The funeral went off well. Tory and Barry's children didn't know the hymns, of course. They couldn't join in, even holding song sheets up in front of them. They'd never heard the tunes. But everyone else (not just Amy and Bethany) sang up quite well. The readings were well chosen. And Megan had somehow managed to frighten the modern vicar into using the traditional words.

'How did you manage that?' asked Tory afterwards.

Megan smiled. 'I warned him that, if he used the modern service, we would pay only the minimum. And if he did what I wanted, we'd make a quite substantial contribution to the church fund.'

'Bravo!' said Tory. She watched her sister walk across to say goodbye to all the people who had come. She seemed so different these days, as if all the anxieties of life had drained away and she was happy. Easy-going, almost. Was it because she'd spent so much time at their mother's side in the last two or three weeks, when all the niggles of two temperaments that don't quite mesh must have seemed unimportant? Surely it couldn't be what Barry had suggested – that Megan was happy now simply because the legacies were finally evened up.

That was so petty. No. It couldn't be that.

Look at her, though, weaving between the members of their mother's old Wednesday morning coffee club to get to Mrs Deloy, who would need thanking properly because she must have caught at least three buses to get the whole way over to Megan's church. So Tory followed. Spotting Anne Taylor making her way determinedly towards her, she took off to the side, and threaded through a knot of people whom she didn't recognise, telling herself a funeral was neither the time nor place to be harangued about a crumbling wall. The house was up for sale in any case. In a short while, with luck, it would no longer be Tory and Megan's problem.

She got through safely. Mrs Deloy and Megan were talking. 'Maybe call in just once or twice a week?' Megan was saying. 'Of course you must fit in the visits to the house at times that suit you. Really, it's just a matter of picking up the fliers that come through the letterbox, and keeping the place looking orderly until the sale's watertight. I don't think that'll be long.'

Mrs Deloy looked from one sister to the other. She didn't smile. Indeed, the look on her face smacked more of curiosity than anything else. Perhaps, thought Tory, in the culture in which Coral Deloy was raised, it was bad form to try to make practical arrangements with mourners at a funeral. So she stepped in. 'It was so good of you to come. Didn't you think the service really suited Mum? Megan's to thank for that.' She turned to her sister. 'No, don't shake your head like that. You know you sorted it all! And it was lovely.' Tory turned back to Mrs Deloy. 'Not only that, but Megan has arranged some gorgeous nibbles in the church hall. You must pop in and have a cup of tea and some of the lovely sandwiches before you even think of trekking home.'

Now Megan laid a hand on Mrs Deloy's arm. 'Speaking of trekking home, I've taken the liberty of fixing you up a lift. One of Mum's Wednesday ladies is driving your way. She was wondering if setting off in about twenty minutes would be any good for you?'

132

The sisters stood exchanging smiles. Tory, at least, knew quite enough about buses to guess how much time would be saved. But Coral Deloy still didn't smile, just stood and searched their faces, seemingly not so much grateful for the sisters' thoughtfulness as curious and watchful.

You could have said that she looked wary, almost.

It was very puzzling.

*

The car lost power three times on the drive to Childon. 'This is quite dangerous,' said Tory as a lorry screeched to a halt behind them on a roundabout.

'You should approach more slowly,' Barry advised, 'and then speed up and stay in third.'

They reached the open road and both of them relaxed again. 'First thing we do,' said Barry, 'is get a new car.'

'Two new cars.'

The children in the back, who had been silenced by the tension in the air, now started up again. 'New cars? Will we be getting money now that Granny's dead?'

'Will they be posh cars? Can we have an Audi? Tom's dad has Audis and they're brilliant.'

'Can it be red? I hate this boring blue thing.'

Barry and Tory waited until the pestering died down, and all three had returned to their texting and screen games. Then Barry said as softly as he could, 'About this money...'

Tory shrugged. 'I don't know. Megan's said nothing and I haven't liked to ask.'

'How long do these things take?'

'Weeks, I should think. Perhaps even longer. I think you get a lump sum first and then the dribs and drabs are tidied up.'

He sighed. 'If you and Megan had still been executors, you would at least have known what to expect.'

'I'm glad Mum changed that. Stephanie was her aunt's executor and says it was a heap of work and just went on for months.'

'You realise those solicitors will snaffle a massive chunk simply for taking the job over?'

'I don't care. I just hate the thought of all that hassle.'

He gave her a fond glance. 'A lot of people claim that they don't care about money. But you are truly easy-come and easy-go about it, aren't you?'

She gave him a quick answering smile. 'Have to be, don't I? What with our crappy record for making and keeping it?'

Lou broke in from the back. 'Is it much further? I think I need to pee.'

'I'm bored,' said Lindy. 'And I didn't want to come in any case. This'll be two whole days, and I was supposed to be getting on with that stupid science project.'

'There was a fancy ice cream shop on that corner! Can we go back?'

'For God's sake!' Barry snapped. 'You only have one grandmother and she only dies once. Just have some patience!'

They sat quietly for a while, not sure if all their mother's threats from yesterday were counting on the journey. Then Ned asked, reasonably enough, 'Why are we going down to Childon anyway?'

Tory leaned back. 'Because that's where my own real dad was buried.'

'Yes, I know that. But why is Granny being buried with him when she was married to Gordon?'

It was a poser. Tory took so much time thinking of an answer that Lindy, too, took up Ned's case. 'Yes, I think it's mean. Gran lived with Gordon for years and years. I never even knew you had another dad till a few years ago. I thought that you just called Grandpa "Gordon" the way Jade calls her mum "Sandy". And I think Granny should have said that she'd be buried with him.'

'Where's Grandpa buried, anyway? asked Lou.

'He isn't,' Ned reminded her. 'He's in that ashes box.'

'Well, why wasn't Gran cremated too? Then they could be together.'

'Or we could sprinkle his ashes on her coffin,' Ned said, remembering what Lou had told him while he was rooting through the cupboard.

'There is a gravestone,' Tory told them weakly. 'It was put up when my dad died and there's a space on it for Elinor's name.'

'Which name? Will they put "Forsyth"? Because that's Gordon's name. That won't look right.'

'I should imagine it will just say "Elinor Mary", along with her dates.'

'Her dates?'

'Not that sort! Dumbo!' And as the children fell to sniggering about the idea of their Granny having dates, Barry turned on the radio and fiddled with one of the knobs until the music played more loudly in the back. Then he said softly to Tory, 'The kids are right, you know. It is the oddest thing, this Childon business. It doesn't seem the least bit normal. Or right. And I can't think why Elinor ever set her heart on it.'

'Perhaps she didn't.'

'What?'

'Well,' Tory said uneasily, 'we only have Megan's word for it, after all. And she has seemed so odd about Gordon lately. Bringing him up all the time. Putting the worst interpretation on everything she remembers.'

'You really think this whole scheme might be Megan's idea, and nothing whatsoever to do with Elinor? I find that hard to credit.'

'Ah,' Tory teased, 'but that's because you're not her sister. Isn't that the turn?'

*

Lindy and Lou sloped off together, scouring the graveyard for a better signal for their phones. Ned ran the other way, to find the hole he guessed must have been dug. Tory went off to find her sister. She could see Malcolm's car. Was Megan in the church? Or already with the vicar, checking the arrangements? There was a good half hour before the time agreed.

Malcolm was in the church porch with his girls. Bethany stood reading notices pinned up behind a boxed, wired frame, and Amy was sitting on the narrow side bench, copying something from one school exercise book into another. Christ, did these girls never stop?

'You made good time,' said Malcolm.

'It's only luck we're here at all,' said Tory. 'The car lost power whenever I changed down. The bloody shit heap!'

Amy and Bethany looked up, not used to hearing quite such colourful language from an adult, especially in a church. Malcolm said, 'It's possible that it's the air control valve. You could try giving it a clean.'

'I wouldn't recognise an air control valve if it had chocolate sprinkles on top. Neither would Barry.'

Malcolm looked at his watch. 'We've got a good twenty minutes. Why don't I take a peep?'

Tory considered. There was no need to upset Barry, who was sensitive about his inability to sort out cars. Look at the hissy fit he'd thrown about that thingummy that fitted the wheel bolt. ('Well, how the hell was

I supposed to know? I'm not a bloody mechanic!') She turned to cunning – and to Ned who, mission accomplished, had come up behind her. 'Ned, sweetie! Run over to your dad and ask him for the car keys.'

'Why? We only just got here. Where are you going now?'

'I'm not going anywhere. It's just there's something in the car I want.'

'What?'

'Stop asking questions! Just go and get the keys!'

'All right,' said Ned. 'Keep your hair on.'

Tory saw Amy and Bethany exchange a glance, and Amy hid a smile. Suppressing irritation, Tory turned to Malcolm. 'If you could take a look at it, that would be very kind.'

*

Barry was wondering what time they'd get away. Would it be sensible to call in at a garage to ask advice about the loss of power? Or should he just insist on taking the wheel, and trust to his driving skills and luck to get them home intact? No point in asking Tory. She always thought that things would work out fine. If he did truly think it wasn't safe, he'd have to say so and he'd also have to be quite firm. Lindy would squawk her head off, determined as she was to get back for Ali's party.

It would be a fight.

Where was the service manual and all that stuff? There might be something on the troubleshooting page. Barry opened the glove compartment. It had been stuffed so full that things spewed out onto the floor: a bobble hat, suntan lotion, two ancient mobiles, half a pair of sunglasses, one lonely sock, a stuffed toy rabbit, nail scissors. And what the hell was that? A desiccated lamb chop bone? Jesus!

No manual, though. But there had been one when they bought the car, he did know that because there'd been that problem when he changed the wheel. A special whatsit that you had to use to undo that last bolt. That had been in the boot. Perhaps he'd thrown the whole lot back in there when he was done, manual and all.

Sighing, he slid off the passenger seat and went round to the back of the car. The boot was as cluttered as usual. Muttering imprecations, Barry set about shifting things from one side to the other: a ratty old blanket; two plastic buckets; empty windscreen fluid bottles; a box of dress-ups.

What was that at the back? Whoopsie! Of all the places to bring Gordon's ashes!

Hastily, Barry pulled what was left of the blanket over the box and tucked it in. He didn't know that Ned had sidled up behind him. He didn't realise Ned had seen. He slammed the boot lid down.

Ned, who had taken several silent steps backwards, now moved forward again. 'Mum says she wants the car keys.'

Barry tossed them over. 'She's welcome to them. Heap of shit!'

*

The Reverend Angela Thirsk had a soft spot for children, thinking they ought to be invited to weddings and christenings and funerals. She'd raised a hackle or two on stubborn brides who'd claimed, 'But I don't want them charging up and down the aisles while I am taking my vows. I'm paying all that money for the service to be filmed, and I don't want it ruined.' More than one future bride had changed her mind about St Edmund's and decided to have her marriage ceremony somewhere else.

The vicar wasn't quite so sure about interments. The funeral service, yes. That was a positive appraisal of a valued life. But standing watching a coffin being lowered into dank, sodden earth was rather more testing.

On the other hand, this was the children's grandmother. It would be much less harrowing than seeing a parent or a brother or sister buried. Even the youngest – Ned, had his mother called him? – could probably handle it. But just to give the young boy something a sight more cheerful to think about before the service began, the vicar called him over. 'Could I ask you to do a little job for me during the ceremony.'

It was to do with petals. She handed him a woven basket, filled to the brim with them. 'If you keep track of that, then when the moment comes I'm going to ask you to pass it round so everyone can sprinkle a few onto your granny's coffin, and say their own little private prayer of goodbye.'

'Like sprinkling ashes?' Ned asked.

The Reverend Thirsk was pleased. So many children nowadays knew nothing of the rituals of life and death. 'That's absolutely right. Like sprinkling ashes.'

'Righty-ho,' Ned said cheerfully. 'I can do that.'

She watched him walk off, swinging the basket rather violently until he realised he was letting loose a trail of petals. Then, like the willing child he seemed to be, he turned around to pick every last one up.

They all stood round the grave. Mats of false plastic grass were spread around to hide the brutal mounds of freshly dug earth that would be shovelled back after. The Reverend Thirsk began with a short prayer, and then went on for quite a while about the strains and virtues of long widowhood. At first Tory barely listened, fixing her eyes on the gravestone's weathered lettering and trying to recall her father's face. But after the word 'widow' had snagged at her consciousness for the umpteenth time, her attention snapped back. She was in time to hear the vicar round up her homily with the triumphant words, 'Together at last.'

Had Megan failed to make it clear to Reverend Thirsk that Elinor had remarried? Probably. If Tory's intuition was correct and this whole jamboree was just her sister's way of cocking a snook at Gordon, then she'd be more than capable of steamrollering through any inconvenience to get her way. Tory recalled once filling in a newspaper quiz, first on her own account, then on her sister's. Tick A if you would be most likely to... Tick B if you would... Tick C if... Tory had ended up with mostly As and earned the character description that began, 'We're not going to say you're feckless, but...'

She had awarded Megan mostly Cs. 'Is there a goal you've never reached? Frankly, we doubt it.'

So Megan had presumably ladled out just enough information to make the vicar assume that John Stuart Brown was Elinor's first, last and only love. Small wonder Megan hadn't asked for Tory's help, and each time it was offered, her sister had declared that everything was well in hand. Not that Tory had minded, to be fair. After all, in what she had assumed would be a massively demanding week, Tory had not only managed to get her hair trimmed and spend an afternoon with Stephanie, she'd even found the time to go to yoga twice. And after all, the dead were dead. They didn't care where, or with whom, their bodies lay forever.

So good for Megan, who was standing just across from her, a daughter on each side and Malcolm behind, handsome and serious in his dark suit. It was, thought Tory, such a pity that the cousins didn't mix more easily at family events. Her three were stubbornly hanging back yards behind Barry and herself (hopefully not texting). The Reverend Thirsk had already hinted twice that they should move closer.

Four men stepped forward to deal out the bands that lowered the coffin steadily into the grave. The vicar said more prayers. Everyone bowed their heads respectfully, except for Ned, who had come forward to see better as the box went down.

And then the Reverend Thirsk favoured them all with a smile. 'Now comes the moment for our personal farewells to Elinor. The rose petal is one of our most potent symbols of love, and Ned here has agreed to help by offering round the basket. As each of us in turn lets our handful of petals fall onto the resting place of this woman we have trusted to God's care, we'll say, either aloud or silently in our own minds, our last few words to her.'

Ned dutifully picked up the basket and stood, unsure of how or where to start. Hastily Barry indicated Megan. Ned hurried around the open grave to her side and offered the basket with both hands, the same way he'd been taught to give his cardboard frankincense to the Infant Lord in his first nativity play. Playing her own role of Chief Mourner to perfection, Megan bestowed on him in turn her saddest smile. Daintily she dipped her fingers into the basket, mouthed a few words and let her bright red petals flutter down. Ned had by then moved on to Malcolm, who did much the same. Amy and Bethany copied them, though Amy's lips stayed tightly closed and Bethany threw just two petals and one blew away.

Gaining confidence, Ned took the somewhat depleted basket past the Reverend Thirsk and back round the grave to his mother. She dipped her fingers in and, looking somewhat startled, threw her petals out over the grave and turned her attention to her fingers. Barry was next. Trying to hide the fact that he despised this sort of gesture, he dipped his hand quite forcibly in the basket, then tossed, not just rose petals, but a deal of rough scrapings that appeared to be mixed in with them, into the grave.

Lindy was not keen either. But she was determined to get to Ali's party so she made a valiant show of digging in the basket, and gathering her own mix of petals and the strange abrasive bits. Already Lou was scooping out her own small contribution. Almost in tandem the two of them threw out their handfuls.

The pattering sound brought Megan forward with a look of horror on her face. She was too late. The Reverend Thirsk had told Ned earlier, 'I think that, at the end, it would be nice if you just tipped the basket so the last few petals can float down.'

Ned shouted, far more loudly than he need, 'Goodbye, then, Grandpa!'

Up went the basket, and half a pound or more of Gordon's pulverised bone matter cascaded noisily onto the lid.

*

'What was that?' It was as if Megan hadn't realised the ceremony wasn't yet over. 'What did you lot just throw into the grave?'

Everyone was puzzled. Then Tory recalled sending Ned back for the car keys just at the moment Barry suddenly remembered pulling the picnic rug over the hidden box. 'It's all right, honestly,' said Tory, though she knew it wasn't, and Barry backed her up. 'Don't worry, Megan.'

The Reverend Thirsk opened her mouth to speak, but Megan cut her short. 'But what was that? What have your family thrown in there? Is it what I think it might be?'

Tory and Barry turned to Ned. 'Is it—?'

'Why not?' said Ned. His face was burning and he turned accusingly to Lou. 'It's your fault. It was you who told me!'

His sister was outraged. 'I told you what?'

'That if they loved each other, Granny and Grandpa should be sprinkled.'

The vicar edged herself forward. 'I wonder if this might be an excellent moment to—'

No one was listening. Megan was glowering at her sister's family across the grave. 'You're telling me you lot have had the nerve to come down here and—'

'Stop it!' snapped Tory. 'Stop right now, Megan! Ned thought that he was doing something thoughtful. Something everyone would like.'

'Like?'

'Yes!' Tory said. 'A loving gesture. Like those stupid rose petals.'

Now Ned looked hurt. So did the Reverend Thirsk. But she reminded herself firmly that people often got upset at burials. She pulled herself together. 'Now I do truly think that—'

Megan ignored her. She was still glaring at her sister over the open grave. 'Your family has a nerve. You don't do anything to help all week. You just sit on your bums as usual, leaving the whole lot to me—'

'That's hardly fair! I offered several times!'

'And then you come down here and take it upon yourselves to hide those—' – words were failing Megan – 'those damn bits under the rose petals.'

'Nobody hid them, Megan! Ned simply thought it would be nice.'

Now Ned was shouting. 'No, I didn't hide them. I tried to stir them in with the rose petals but they were too heavy. They're like that cat litter we used to get.'

Megan was pointing over the grave like a witch starting on a curse. 'I don't care what they're like! I want them out!'

'Oh, lighten up!' said Tory. 'It's perfectly all right for them to be in there. The two of them were married, after all, for thirty years.'

'Twenty-eight!' Megan screamed. 'I told you before! It was only twenty-eight years!'

Malcolm broke out of his paralysis and took his wife by the arm. 'Steady on, Megan.' He knew her grand hysteria about Gordon's ashes stemmed from his own distortion of the truth, and realised it was his responsibility to bring this dreadful performance to a swift end. 'Leave it for now. You'll just upset the girls.'

'Bugger the girls!'

Amy and Bethany, who had been interested enough, now appeared riveted. Was this their mother swearing? The Reverend Thirsk forced her way forward. Spreading her arms in a peace-giving fashion, she tried once more. 'I really, really do think that the very best thing we can all do is—'

'I am not leaving here,' snapped Megan, 'till all those bits of kitty litter have been taken out of this grave.'

'I'm not sure that...'

'I mean it!' Megan warned. 'I will be happy to stay here all night. And if those men come back and try to shovel earth onto the lid, I shall jump down there and I'll bloody throw it back.'

'Oh, please!' said Tory. 'Now you're being quite ridiculous. And I am taking my family home.'

'Do,' Megan said. 'I only wish you hadn't come at all.'

'Don't think that you're the only one to wish that.' Tory put out a hand to pull Ned closer, then she led her little troop away from the graveside.

The Reverend Thirsk tried one more time. 'I do rather wonder if...'

But absolutely no one in Tory's family heard, and nobody in Megan's paid the slightest attention.

12.

The car ran perfectly through several unavoidable downward gear changes. 'Odd, that,' said Barry after the third roundabout. 'Seems to be fine now.'

Tory was not going to say a word, but Ned explained, 'That's because Uncle Malcolm fixed it for us. He cleaned some valve, or spark plug, or something.'

'Oh, did he?'

'Just be pleased,' Tory rebuked her irritated husband. 'He's saved the cost of a car servicing – and maybe all our lives.'

'Frankly, after that ghastly scene, I'd just as soon be dead.'

And so the topic was breached. And trusting that the music of all their offspring in the back was turned up to the usual ruinous levels, the two of them settled to the discussion. 'So what was all that about?'

'I don't know,' Barry said. 'Your guess is as good as mine.'

'I know she's got her knickers in a twist about poor Gordon. But I still find it very hard to fathom why simply learning that we had more than our fair share of handouts would turn her quite so venomous.'

'That was an awful business. I can't imagine what that vicar thought.'

'Serves her right,' Tory said. 'All of that crap with rose petals. Soppy damn woman.'

'And what was all that mad guff about Elinor being a chaste and saintly widow for so many years? The way you've always told it, your mother's feet had barely touched the ground after your father's funeral before she'd married Gordon.'

'The whole thing is a total mystery.'

'So are you going to ask your sister what the hell is in her head?'

'No, I am bloody not. I am not going to speak to her until I get a fulsome apology.'

'An apology? From Megan?'

'She was extremely rude and hurtful to poor Ned.'

Barry was more inclined to take the view that Ned deserved it. He'd been both sneaky and disobedient in snaffling the ashes. But he said nothing except, 'So what'll happen now?'

'Nothing,' said Tory. 'Since Megan is no longer an executor, she can't stop anything. Russell Powers Solicitors presumably get on with sorting the will. And in the end we'll get whatever we are getting, and that's the end of it.'

'You plan to stay at daggers drawn?'

'Unless she says she's sorry.'

'Blimey.'

They drove in silence for a while. Then Barry said, 'So what about the rest of Gordon's ashes? I take it that you don't intend to keep them in the car for ever?'

'No. No, I don't. I'm driving back tomorrow and I'm going to dig the rest of them into the earth on the grave.'

'You have to be joking!'

'No. That's what I'm going to do. My sister isn't going to bully me. It's not my fault she's somehow got it in her head that Gordon was some sort of fiend. Mum shouldn't have been buried with my dad. It isn't right. I should have said so sooner, except I was so glad to leave the business of arranging things to her. Ned had the right idea, and I am going to follow through.'

'Suppose you're seen? I'm sure it's probably illegal, or sacrilegious, or something – tampering with a grave.'

'I shall pretend that I am planting lots of forget-me-nots.'

He glanced across. She had that stubborn look upon her face that he knew only too well.

'Right, then,' he said. 'Good thing that Malcolm fixed the car. And we had better fill up.'

*

The packaged urn showed up on the doorstep only a few nights later. When they had finished laughing, Barry asked Tory, 'So what now?'

Tory picked up the cream-coloured plastic tub and studied the label again. *Presumed Cremated Remains, Identity Unknown, Recovered from Childon Cemetery.* 'I could just post them back.'

144

'There's an idea,' he said. 'Instead of resting in peace, the last two or three handfuls of poor Gordon could spend the first few years of eternity being posted between two warring sisters.'

She grinned. 'It is a bit ridiculous, isn't it? I suppose I could drive down to Childon yet again to dig it in with the rest.'

'Yes, it'll give you a chance to water your forget-me-nots.'

She stared at the pale, gritty stuff he'd tipped on the newspaper spread on the kitchen table. 'It is an awfully long way to drive, just for these few last handfuls. Couldn't we scatter them somewhere nearer here where Gordon liked being?'

'Where? At his accountant's? Or his stockbroker's?'

That gave her an idea. 'I know! We'll shove them in the wall.'

'What wall?'

'The one he wouldn't fix. The wall that Mrs Taylor kept on pestering Mum about after Gordon died. We'll just sneak round to the house and tip the bits in. Gordon won't show up in all the crumbling.'

'I thought the house was sold.'

'It is. But I drove past it yesterday and it's still empty. It won't take long, and if the new people show up I'll claim I'm looking round my childhood garden one last time.'

'It's not your childhood garden. Gordon and your mother only moved in there a few years ago.'

'They won't know that, though, will they?'

He sighed. 'Let's hope that you're not spotted by that fusspot neighbour. If you go pouring the last of Gordon into her party wall, she isn't going to be pleased.'

*

Anne Taylor was in the garden in a flash. 'What are you doing, Tory?'

Hastily Tory dropped the freshly emptied urn out of sight on her own side. 'Nothing.'

'I had hoped that your family might have been considerate enough to get this wall repaired before you put the house on the market.'

'Oh,' Tory told her vaguely, 'Megan's been looking after everything to do with the sale. But I do think the wall was mentioned, so I expect that something will get done soon.'

'Well, that will be a relief.' Anne Taylor nodded over towards her previous neighbour's kitchen window. 'Are you here to give a hand to Mrs Deloy?'

'Mrs Deloy?'

'She has been coming in every few days just to check round. I generally take her a cup of tea.'

'That's very good of you.'

Anne Taylor sniffed. 'I think that some of us have a rather better idea than others of what it means to be neighbourly. You take this wall—'

'I'm sure,' interrupted Tory, 'that if my mother had only lived a tiny bit longer...'

Mercifully the phone began to ring in Mrs Taylor's house, and as she hurried back to pick it up before it switched to answer phone, Tory snatched up the urn and vanished round the other side of the house.

*

The front door was unlocked, so Tory pushed it open. Mrs Deloy was standing a little further down the hall, tipping a handful of curry house and pizza fliers into a rubbish bag. 'Oh, hello, Tory. You quite startled me.'

'Sorry.' Tory's steps echoed. 'What happened to the carpet?'

'The buyers wanted it away. They didn't like the colour, and didn't want the bother of getting rid of it themselves.' She straightened up. 'Megan was full of it when she rang me. I'm surprised she didn't tell you.'

'She hasn't told me anything,' admitted Tory. 'Since Mum was buried she's been in a frightful snit.'

Probably found out about the will, thought Mrs Deloy. But it was not for her to raise the question of the skewed inheritance. So she said blandly, 'I thought you two seemed to be getting on a good deal better than usual...'

Perhaps, thought Tory, a long-term cleaning lady comes to think of each of her families as a soap opera. If so, this was the final episode of this one. There was no need for discretion now. The new owners might ask Mrs Deloy to stay (so long as they were happier with her colour than with the colour of the carpet). But this was surely the last time she'd have a place in Tory's life.

And it was such a good story. Why not tell her?

'Yes. We all thought the funeral went brilliantly. But the interment on the following day turned out a nightmare. Megan began a bloody shouting match over the grave. The poor vicar didn't know where to look.'

'Your Megan? Shouting?'

'Yes, she went wild at Ned. He threw a handful of Gordon's ashes onto the coffin and Megan practically accused him of desecrating his Granny's grave. She even threatened to jump in and fling soil back at anyone who tried to fill in the hole before the ashes had been taken out.'

'Never!'

'She did. It was the weirdest thing I've ever seen.'

Mrs Deloy could understand perfectly well why Megan was hair-triggered to lose her temper with one of Tory's offspring at a graveside service. That Ned boy was a menace, and in between the funeral and the interment, she'd probably found out about the will. Mrs Deloy now clutched her dustpan closer, even more anxious than before that she had failed to step in on that fateful morning when the will was being discussed. She could have spoken up. She could have said, 'Elinor, as I was getting the vacuum out from under the stairs, I couldn't help overhearing. Are you quite sure you want things that way? It does seem so unfair.' But people's lives are, after all, their own – though she should never have allowed that Hatcher woman to bully her into witnessing that shocking document the very next day.

All done now, though, and it was not her business anyway. So she trod carefully. 'Could it be stress? The two of you have had a time of it recently.'

'Megan seemed perfectly all right moments before. And then she just went mental.'

'Couldn't her husband stop her?'

'Malcolm? He didn't even seem to try, though he looked mortified. He just kept staring at his feet and looking guilty.'

The word had sprung unbidden from her mouth. But suddenly Tory realised it was true. She hadn't thought about it before. But Malcolm had looked guilty.

Mrs Deloy stuck safely to the role of peacemaker. 'Still, dear. Two funerals hard on one another's heels. It is a horrible shock.'

'Hardly a shock. We'd known for weeks and weeks that Mum was dying.'

Mrs Deloy could not resist one tiny feeler out towards the truth. 'Something about your mother's new will, perhaps?'

'I can't believe that. Megan's done more than well enough for herself!'

Mrs Deloy knew what she thought. Yes, it was true that Megan and Malcolm were well heeled. They didn't need more money. But it was understandable that she'd be in a snit with Tory being given so much more. If Tory couldn't sympathise with that, there was no point in trying to discuss it.

She gathered up the cleaning things that she'd brought with her. 'Well, dear, I'm sorry if there's trouble in the family. But I did promise Winston that I'd try to get back before he has to go off for the night shift.'

Tory had sensed the tension, and she regretted saying what she had to someone who had no doubt always had to work for every single penny. 'Right, then. I absolutely mustn't keep you. But thank you one more time for always being so very good to Mum.'

'It was a pleasure. I was very fond of Elinor – until the end.'

A slightly curious way of putting it, thought Tory, as she said goodbye.

*

Malcolm jammed the trowel into the soft soil of the grave and found himself unearthing what looked like scores and scores of tiny dog's teeth. Or pale kitty litter.

Then he realised. Oh, Jesus! Suppose Megan saw! She would go mental. Megan would guess at once that Tory had been back to dig in every last ounce of their stepfather's remains. Probably from spite.

No, that was not at all fair. For Malcolm knew that Gordon had every right to share a resting place with Elinor. He'd asked around. More people than he'd reckoned had parents who had lived through marriages beyond their first. Most were divorced, and so the question of whom they chose to lie beside for all eternity was not an issue. It was definitely not Spouse Number One. But he had heard about a couple of widows and one widower who had remarried, and in every case they had been buried with the recent partner.

So he felt dreadful. He'd been very wrong in telling Megan such a lie about Gordon Forsyth. The idea had come in such a sudden flash. (He'd practically seen it up in neon: *Need a quick rescue? Try this!*) But she had been so desperately aggrieved. Small wonder she had baulked at having even a few handfuls of her stepfather's ashes inside her mother's grave. The sweeping of the coffin lid had been a right performance. First they'd had to persuade a most unwilling Reverend Thirsk to send for a dustpan and brush. They'd kept her waiting twenty minutes more, till Megan was satisfied the grave was clear. And after that he'd had to write that over-generous cheque to smooth the woman's feathers.

Once they were home the fuss had dragged on – sorting out the mess of battered petals, mucky soil and desiccated remains. Since Megan wouldn't let the little bag of it inside the house, he'd done it in the garage. (Malcolm had taken the job upon himself partly from guilt, and partly to keep his half-demented wife away from something she found so enraging.) But in the end it had been done. He had suggested using one of their firm's boxes for the delivery to her sister's house. But she'd turned that idea down flat. God knows where she had found the plastic urn, but she was quite determined to put the filtered ashes into something Tory couldn't criticise. (The mood that she was in, his wife might easily have murdered some poor stranger and booked his body into the crematorium simply to lay her hands on the right sort of urn.)

He thought about confessing. All the time. But he was chicken – far too lily-livered to explain he'd made the whole boiling up. Regarded in the cold light of regret, it was a hateful thing to have done, and he could not imagine trying to explain how he had tried to save himself from one small dent in his own reputation by such black slander on another man.

And caused his wife so much pain. Since that slick lie, he'd watched her sliding every last family group photograph that featured Gordon out of its frame to replace it with one that didn't. He'd seen her grit her teeth each time one of the children so much as mentioned their grandfather. And she'd spent hours trawling through her childhood diaries in search of ancient grudges to resurrect. She'd been obsessed enough to let her usual habits slip. As often as not, Amy and Bethany's homework had gone unsupervised. Nobody appeared to keep an eye on how often or how long Bethany practised her oboe most evenings. And in the office, Malcolm had come across a heap of unpaid invoices that Megan hadn't even chased.

No, she was not herself. His only hope was that his mother-in-law had come up trumps and sorted out the will sufficiently for Megan to at least be sure her mother truly loved her. Then, perhaps, everything to do with Gordon might finally calm down. It certainly wouldn't help to let her know about these fresh bits of crushed bone (could you in any real way call them 'fresh'?) he'd just found in the soil on the grave.

So back to deception. And he'd had more than enough of that. He saw himself essentially as an honest man. He'd made one silly mistake along the line – having that mad idea to shunt a portion of one of his own legal bills onto Miss Tallentire. For heaven's sake! How was he to have known that she was Gordon's godmother, and some word that James Harrow had presumably let drop had somehow worked its way back round to Gordon?

And he felt guilty about Tory, too. His sister-in-law had come down here to plant forget-me-nots, and then presumably a second time to lay the last remains of Gordon under the surface of this soil. Meanwhile, the sisters weren't on speaking terms. How long would that go on? Oh, grim, grim, grim! How could some ancient whisper about a minor fiddle that was discussed, but never even took place, and one quick panicked lie, fetch down such misery? God, it was so unfair! Almost unreal!

He heard the scrunch of gravel. Turning, he saw his wife step sideways onto the grass, brushing dirt from her fingers. 'That's Tory's horrid cheap offerings on the compost heap – where they belong!'

Thank heavens that she hadn't noticed all the scratchy grey bits in the soil while she was ripping out her sister's plants. 'Do me a favour,' he said, before she came too close. 'Can you stroll round to that corner shop and get me a bottle of fizz?'

'You don't want any help?'

'No, no. I'm fine. I'll get these periwinkles planted.' Malcolm pulled one or two out of the box. Good thing they offered lots of ground cover. Most of the kitty-litterish bits seemed to be at the top end, away from where the forget-me-nots had been before they were torn out. By the time Megan came back, he'd have the periwinkles there, all safely spread.

13.

It was a surprisingly short time before the thick brown envelope from Russell Powers, Solicitors, fell through the letter box. 'My God!' said Barry, looking at the figures. 'How much did the man have?'

'That isn't even all of it.' Tory was reading the accompanying letter. 'This is the first tranche, and the rest will come when every last thing's settled.'

'It's an enormous amount. I've never seen so much money! Gordon must have been far, far richer than we thought.' He grinned. 'That, or the new solicitor Elinor hired to rejig the will got things the wrong way.'

It was a joke, but Tory still responded sourly. 'Well if she did, and Megan keeps on in the way she has, I won't be hurrying to sort it out.'

For Megan had not been in touch. Not once. At first, Tory wasn't surprised. But lack of contact persisted even through Tory's birthday. Megan didn't ring, or even send a card.

Tory became uneasy. 'What will we do at Christmas?'

'Christmas? We don't spend Christmas with her family anyway.'

'We send a card. And presents to the girls.'

'So do that. Send a card. And presents for the girls.'

'No. No, I won't. Not unless she does first.' Catching the look on his face, she said, 'And don't you tell me that I'm being silly!'

'I wouldn't dare.'

'Good thing, because I'm not.'

Was she? He couldn't work it out. On the one hand, her sister had behaved disgracefully at the interment. And yet, so what? Ned was robust enough to take a bit of shrieking from a relative. Even if his feelings were hurt, he'd known damn well that no one wanted him to meddle with those ashes. He was in the wrong.

And Megan had made all the arrangements for the funeral and the separate burial. He and Tory hadn't worried about that, guessing (presumably quite rightly) that Megan would find it easier to make decisions without the bother of discussing things. So Tory had been justifiably incensed to be accused over the grave in Childon of not pulling her weight. Each time she'd been in touch ('You're sure we can't do anything to help?') Megan had claimed that she had everything in hand. He'd overheard enough to know that was a fact. Still, he was forced to recognise that he and Tory had had an easy time of it because of Megan's efforts. He'd not been inconvenienced at all, and Tory had enjoyed a most relaxing week before the funeral. She'd actually bragged about getting to yoga, the hairdresser and the Turkish baths all in those short few days.

Should he perhaps drive over there and talk to Megan?

Better not!

But Malcolm, now… After all, he had helped out Malcolm, hadn't he? He had persuaded Tory to ask her mother to adjust the will. If things kept on this way, he'd phone and maybe make another date to meet his brother-in-law again at Howey's (now that that snotty girl behind the bar had moved on somewhere else). Between the two of them, they might be able to sort out this mess. Malcolm could probably explain why Megan was in such a state about her stepfather. Once they knew that, then Tory might be able to take a step towards conciliation.

Yes, he'd do that. But not right now because the whole caboodle might just sort itself out without any help from him. Megan and Tory had, after all, had frosty patches before. And life in any case went on the same with or without his sister and brother-in-law. The four of them had never really been close. They'd not invited Megan and Malcolm to their Easter party, after all. And Christmas would seem much the same without that stiff and formal little visit when Megan came by in her best skirt and blouse to drop a box of beautifully wrapped presents at their house, and pick up anything they might have managed to rustle up in a great hurry for her lot.

Leave it till after Christmas. Then, if the two of them were still not on speakers, he would do something about it. Right now, he had a thousand things to do. Now that the bulk of the money had arrived, he wanted to buy two brand new cars, replace the boiler, sort out the leaking garage roof and maybe even choose a holiday.

Yes, he most definitely had plans.

*

Malcolm stared at the letter he'd pulled from the thick brown envelope, then read it through again. No, he was not mistaken. It clearly stated this amount was almost all that Megan should expect from Elinor Forsyth's estate. A further transfer might be made a short time in the future, but that would simply be as a result of insignificant sums trickling in late. Meanwhile, could Megan sign and date and promptly return the enclosed form, confirming receipt of the solicitor's cheque.

Malcolm stared at the amount again. Was that all? Either his parents-in-law had been a damn sight poorer than the whole world thought, or something had gone very, very wrong.

Thank God he'd opened up the envelope before it got to Megan. He'd just been desperately curious. (And she'd ripped open enough of his Premium Bond prize envelopes when he was not yet home for him to be assured she'd understand.) But now he'd seen this paltry – almost insulting – cheque, the best thing he could do was hide it from her for a day or two. Perhaps the changes Elinor had made had been a lot more radical than he'd envisaged and, to avoid more niggling, or even from sheer exasperation, she'd left the bulk of the estate directly to the grandchildren. Perhaps more letters would arrive tomorrow, but this time for them. That was quite possible. He'd wait a day or two and then, if nothing came, he would track down a copy of the will to find out what had happened to all the money. That should be simple enough since, once a will had been confirmed in probate, it became a public document.

Only then need he show his wife this letter and the cheque. Until he knew the facts, he simply couldn't face the sleepless nights, his wife's consuming anguish and all the questions nobody could answer. 'How could my mother do that? Who got the bulk of the estate? Did she decide to leave it all to charity at the last minute? Or has it all fetched up in Tory's grasping fist?'

There would be grief if it had! Of course he recognised that might not be his sister-in-law's fault. Tory may well have done what Barry promised he would ask her to do – spoken to Elinor about adjusting the will to make it more fair. But Tory had never been one to put the time and effort into being tactful, and Elinor had never truly forgiven Megan for casting such a pall on Gordon's welcome to the house. It was a well-known fact that people always nursed a grudge against the ones that they themselves had wronged, and surely Elinor must have felt guilty at heart for being so insensitive to Megan's feelings as a grieving child.

Perhaps she'd pounced upon this opportunity to take offence, and shown her resentment with the startlingly small amount in this solicitor's cheque.

Except it didn't make sense. If you were going to take a huff against a daughter for demanding more, you wouldn't leave them a weird amount like this. You'd cut them off with something rounded and symbolic – what your solicitor might tell you was the modern-day equivalent of the traditional penny.

No. If there was nothing almost breathtakingly substantial for the girls – and Tory's children too – then something had gone very wrong.

It would be hard, though, to persuade his wife. Megan would take one look at this and there would be such wailing and gnashing of teeth as this house had never yet seen. It would make what he'd told her about Gordon fade in the background utterly. She would be staring at the final proof that, though her stepfather had so disliked her, her mother must have hated her even more.

Oh, God. She would be uncontrollable. The girls would be appalled.

He heard her key in the front door.

Hastily Malcolm stuffed the letter and the cheque back in the envelope and ran upstairs. Unzipping the moth-proof cover that protected his dress suit, he slid it into the breast pocket. The suit had been dry cleaned only the week before, and they had not a single formal event marked on the calendar. It would be safe there.

He heard her calling from the hall. 'Malcolm? You home?'

Standing before the mirror, he dropped his shoulders, willing himself to breathe more deeply, and be calm.

'Yes, I'm back, Megan. Just on my way down.'

*

So there it was, in black and white. Elinor's last will and testament. He read it through enough times to be absolutely sure. No legacies to any of the grandchildren. A vast chunk – ludicrously large – directly to Victoria. And then what little was left was shared between her and her sister.

Nothing could be more unfair.

Now he would have to let poor Megan know. He'd have to snaffle the morning post, retrieve that envelope from his dress suit pocket, and hand the whole stack to her when she got back from Waitrose. 'Sorry, I couldn't help but open that one.'

Would she go ashen? Might she even faint?

In fact, she did neither, just looked baffled at first. 'Not sure I get it...' She read the covering letter through again, more slowly, just as he himself had done. 'Is this it?'

'Yes. Or so it seems.'

'You don't think there's been some mistake?'

'I doubt it, Megan.'

'But what about the money for the girls?'

'I suppose she dropped those legacies.'

Megan looked puzzled. 'Dropped them?' She looked up. 'Do you suppose she dropped them just because I mentioned to her that they weren't quite fair?'

'Possibly.'

'But what about the rest? Where's all the money?'

'I suspect it's gone to Tory.'

'The whole lot?' She waved the cheque. 'Apart from this?'

'I rather think so.'

Megan stared at him. 'I've never heard of such a thing. How could a mother split things up so one of her daughters gets the whole damn lot, and the other gets practically nothing?'

He thought it best to cover his recent tracks on the will-sleuthing front. 'Megan, we're not entirely sure yet that she did that.'

'Oh, I am,' she said. 'There's no way that my mother was the sort to leave her money to a charity. It would be family or nothing. So if none of the money's come to me, it's gone to Tory.'

He pointed to the figure on the cheque. 'It isn't none, exactly.'

'Compared to what we know that Gordon had, this isn't anything.'

He didn't argue. He just stood there waiting for the storm.

*

It never happened. Days went by and there were no tears, no complaints, no anguished questioning of how, and why. From time to time Malcolm would put out a feeler. 'It does seem very odd...' And she'd just shrug. 'Mum's money. So Mum's choice.'

'You don't think you should phone your sister? Maybe you could find out a little more from Tory about what made Elinor do it?'

'I shan't be speaking to Tory till I've had a full apology for her family's behaviour at the grave.'

'That isn't going to happen.' He tried a little cunning. 'And Elinor's just proved she didn't deserve any real loyalty and concern on your part even when she was alive, let alone once she was dead.'

'Then I am better off without the pack of them.'

And she did seem to be. For several weeks he still expected her to crack – suddenly burst into tears, or phone Russell Powers in a fury, demanding an explanation as to why they'd let a dying, drug-addled lady sign such a manifestly unfair will. The second and last cheque arrived, for such a small amount he had to take it off her, fearing that she would tear it up in sheer contempt. But all the rest of the time she just got on with things. Her efforts in the firm were once more undiminished, and her concentration fine. She had gone back to watching over the girls, checking their homework, noting how long they practised, knowing where they were. Their lives reverted to the old routine they'd shared before her mother first fell ill, and Gordon died. Tranquil and organised, with more than enough money from their own efforts to see them easily through their days.

They were all most content.

*

He saw the car the moment it sailed round the corner. It sped past silently, a sleek and pale green ghost, and through the windscreen Malcolm saw Tory's face.

So much for any hidden hope he might have had that Tory might be sitting on the money, wondering if she should offer Megan half. That car had cost the earth.

Curious, he finished everything he had to do in town, then drove off in the direction Tory had been driving, towards Staines Crescent. He parked on the corner, and strolled along just far enough to see the smooth green car parked on the roadside outside their house.

In Tory's narrow driveway there was another exactly the same, but in the brightest red.

And a *For Sale* sign.

He drove home thoughtfully, wondering how to tell Megan. He still was not convinced this wouldn't be the final straw.

But he was wrong again.

*

'Moving? I'm not surprised. Anyone in their right mind would want to get out of that drab, poky little house as soon as they could afford it.'

'It's not that drab and poky. It's only looks that way because it's grubby and cluttered, and nobody ever bothers to put anything away.'

'And two brand new expensive cars? Let's hope that this time Barry can be bothered to get them serviced.'

Malcolm cracked. Gripping his wife by the wrists, he forced her to face him. 'Listen,' he said. 'You have to talk to me. You have to explain. Your mother treats you like a piece of shit. Your sister takes advantage of a graveside quarrel to hide from having to talk to you about the most iniquitous and spiteful family will. And look at you! You're as calm as a Hindu cow.'

'Calm as *what*?'

He brushed her evident amusement aside. 'You know exactly what I mean. This isn't natural, and I want an explanation. Now.'

She tried to shake him off. 'Malcolm, the girls will be back any moment.'

'Bugger the girls!' he said.

Reminded of the shocking thing she'd shouted while beside the grave, she'd burst out laughing. Releasing one of her wrists, he reached across to unlock the front door latch. 'The girls will manage. You come along with me.'

She let herself be pulled upstairs, and pushed down on the bed. He left her for only long enough to shoot the small door bolt they hadn't bothered with since even Bethany grew old enough to knock. Then he lay down beside her. 'This is the plan. First we are going to do it. Then you can explain. And I'm not letting you get up again until I'm satisfied.'

She gave him quite a flirty look. 'What sort of satisfied…?'

They heard the front door bang before they'd finished, and footsteps up the stairs. There was a knock, and instantly the door handle rattled. 'Go away!' roared Malcolm. 'Your mum and I are busy. We will be out soon.'

They listened to the giggling on the stairs, and then got back to it. When they were done, he plumped the pillows up for her and said, 'Will it take long for you to tell me everything that's in your mind? Should I go down first and make tea?'

'No, no.' She bunched her hair up and then let it drop. 'There's nothing much to say. I don't feel anything, except more free. We didn't need the money, after all. In fact, I've always very much enjoyed working to earn what we already have.'

'But for them to have cut our family out of pretty well all the inheritance!'

'I wasn't nice to Gordon,' Megan reminded him. 'And in return, it seems he wasn't nice to me. It was quite horrible to find out he'd been giving all that loot to Tory. But now I'm glad that Mum's done just the same. If she had left me a fair share, it would have still been money that came through to me from Gordon, and I'd have felt I maybe should rethink my view of him if I accepted it. And I don't want to do that. Actually, I'm quite enjoying clinging to my low opinion of the man.'

'Really?'

'Yes, really.'

'But what about your mother? Don't try to tell me that you want to cherish a low view of her.'

'I do. I do.' If anything, Megan sounded eager. 'You wouldn't understand. You just adored your mother, and she was a generous-hearted woman. You've always said she loved you unreservedly, and she was kind to everyone she met. You can have no idea what it was like for me to grow up in a house where I was always the piece of grit in the machine.' She shook her head as though still somewhat baffled. 'And with a mother who openly resented my feelings after Dad died. You can't imagine how it felt to see her face go taut and cold each time I made it obvious I couldn't love a total stranger from the moment he showed up, like Tory could.'

'I always knew—'

She hadn't finished, though. 'You never had to grow up well aware that you were the least loved child, and had a mother who cared for herself far more than she loved you. My God! I spent so many years trying to force my mother into being fair with both of us.' Megan let out a short, harsh laugh. 'As if that would have proved a thing! God, what a fool I was!' Now she was bundling up her hair again. 'It's actually quite nice to feel I owe her no warm thoughts at all. As I said, I feel set free.'

'Blimey.'

They sat in silence till they heard the footfalls coming closer up the stairs and a soft clattering outside the door.

'Out soon!' called Malcolm. 'Just be patient, please.'

They heard cascades of giggles. Then, 'No need,' called Amy. 'Bethany and I can guess exactly what you're doing in there, and we have brought you up a tray of tea. We'll leave it here, outside.'

The giggling started up again, and grew a little noisier as Amy and Bethany chased one another down the stairs, back to the kitchen.

'Well,' Malcolm said. 'I must say that we have the nicest girls.'

'We do,' said Megan. 'And we need nothing else. That's why I can't be bothered to even get in touch with Tory and ask her if she wants to put things right.'

14.

Her sister, meantime, didn't want to put things right because she didn't realise they were wrong. Tory was simply waiting for Megan to snap back from the twisted way in which she'd dealt with Elinor's death, and come to her senses again about poor Gordon. She expected the phone to ring any day. Either, she reckoned, it would be Megan herself ('Tory, I have been thinking about things...') or maybe Malcolm. ('Tory, I need a favour. I know that Megan was outrageous at the funeral. But if you could bring yourself to put out the first little feeler...')

But they would have to make at least that much of an effort. Until then, Tory would just get on with spending. While Barry decided on the cars, and toyed with the idea of private pensions, Tory went looking for another house. It was annoying that the appointment times fixed by estate agents always seemed to conflict with yoga and pilates. And there was something wrong with almost all the places she saw. Too near to this. Too far from that. Too bourgeois. Too much glass. They went back twice to view the one she thought most likely, chewing on the idea all through one evening only to find next morning that the owner had withdrawn the house from sale. That had annoyed Tory so much that she determined to spend the day with Stephanie at Bramley Turkish Baths.

'That means you'll miss the test drive for the car I think you'd like,' Barry had warned.

'I don't care,' Tory said. 'So long as what you get me in the end doesn't have to keep going back to be fixed.'

'It'll be new, Tory. So of course it won't have to keep going back to be fixed.'

It did, though. First it was something strange to do with the door locks. Then it was taken in again because of something the man at the showroom claimed was a faulty solenoid. After that, it was dud batteries. Nobody managed to adjust the dashboard clock so it stopped gaining minutes every day. In fact, the car spent more time in the garage than the rust bucket they'd been driving before, and even when the glitches were all ironed out, it seemed the bloody thing had to go back again simply because she'd scratched it pulling into their narrow driveway.

'So what? It's just a little mark along the paintwork. What does it matter?'

'Tory, this is a most expensive car. We have to get it sorted.'

'I don't see why. The old one had far deeper scratches along both the sides, and no one ever bothered.'

'This is different.'

So was the brand new boiler they put in, once Tory had decided that looking for a better house was too much work. Admittedly the old one had coughed and spluttered, with some dud pilot light that blew out in east winds. But when the plumber came to put in the new one, there was a heap of trouble. 'Your venting system isn't up to current standards, I'm afraid. And, Mrs Challoner, I know you're going to find this hard to credit, but up till now you've had no actuators on your manifold.'

Could all those men have taken longer, or have made more mess? And even then the heating didn't seem much better, though somewhat quieter. And some new safety widget meant they could no longer get the steaming baths that they both loved. 'Pain up the arse,' said Barry. 'We should have stuck with the old one.'

Tory felt much the same about the ruby red sofa she had bought on impulse, thinking they'd soon be moving to a larger house. It was enormous. She had to twist her body sideways to get around it at one end, and at the other it stopped the living room door from fully opening. The children, however, adored it. Always, before, they had ignored the shiny wipeable faux-leather sofa in front of the television, preferring to stay in their bedrooms with their laptops, or, if they came downstairs at all, to slump in the ancient corduroy bean bags Barry had kept from college, or sprawl on the floor. Now they spent hours lazing in companionable heaps on this plush ruby monster that had taken over the family room, spilling their drinks on it, hoarding their piles of greasy peanuts on its capacious arms and making Tory wish she'd had the sense to leave a small deposit at the shop till she was sure the sofa was exactly what she wanted, or that a house move was definitely on the cards.

As for the visit to the private school, that was a nightmare. Neither of them had put their heart into the notion of getting the children to switch schools, but Tory felt they should at least consider the idea. So she made the appointment, and frittered away a good part of the day before, considering what to wear. Then she remembered Barry's good suit was at the cleaners, so she had to rush down there. (Her brand new car was in the garage once again, and Barry was at work.) Her only pair of decent shoes were badly scuffed, but there was nothing to be done about that. Shoe shopping was a nightmare.

Heigh ho. Brazen it out.

The head of school could not have been more pleasant with the two of them. It was the questions they were asked that made them uncomfortable. Lindy's results, it seemed, would land her in the lowest sets for almost every subject. How did they think their daughter would feel about that? This would be no reflection on her capabilities, no, not at all. They mustn't think that. It was simply the result of Lindy having followed up till now a somewhat watered-down syllabus. 'Here, we are proud to teach above the standard. Well above, in fact.'

There was a problem with the languages as well. For Lindy had no Latin, and had dropped French two years before in favour of Dramatic Arts. The interview dragged on until the killer question came. 'So tell me, Mr and Mrs Challoner. How do your girls themselves feel about coming here?'

It was all over. Tory said something bland about her daughters gradually coming round to the idea of being parted from old friends. Barry chipped in to support her. Neither admitted to the noisy scene the previous week. 'I am not going to that snobby school! They're freaks! All poncing round in stupid nanny skirts! You sign me on there and I'll run away!'

'You won't get me there, either!'

'Or me,' said Ned, as if he hadn't realised that it was a girls' school.

Back in the car park, Tory said to Barry, 'Well, at least we tried.'

'Not very hard,' said Barry. 'That woman had a pickle up her arse. I didn't take to her at all.' He glanced at the clock on the dashboard. 'Sweetie, it's only twelve. Shall we cheer ourselves up with a nice lunch?'

'Yes, please,' said Tory, and they went off to Forley's, where they drank champagne.

*

Tory bumped into Coral Deloy outside the supermarket. Elinor's former cleaning lady was carrying several heavy-looking bags of shopping, so though Tory was embarrassed at the idea of letting this woman, in particular, see her extraordinarily swish new car, she still felt obliged to say, 'Can I give you a lift? It wouldn't be the least trouble.'

Mrs Deloy put the bags down on the tarmac. 'No, really, Tory. That's very kind of you, but this stuff's not for me. I've just been shopping for one of my gentlemen who's not quite steady on his pins.' She pointed. 'He'll be waiting in the car.'

'I hope you're well.' Tory did a quick brain search for Mrs Deloy's husband's name and luckily it came up promptly. 'Both you and Winston.'

Mrs Deloy looked pleased. 'We are, Tory. Yes, I'm glad to say we are. And how about you and your sister and the families?'

'I'm all right,' Tory said. 'And so are Barry and the children. But as for Megan and her gang, I've no idea, because we're not on speakers.'

'Still?' Mrs Deloy looked anxious. 'Oh, Tory, dear! She is your sister. I really would have hoped you would have got things sorted out by now.'

'There's nothing to sort out. Megan just stayed in that great snit about the funeral.'

'It wasn't about the funeral, Tory.'

The tone was one of sad rebuke and, irritated by the petty niggle, Tory responded, 'All right then, the interment.'

Clearly, once Coral Deloy stopped working for a family she lost all habits of deference. 'I think you know it wasn't that either, Tory. It was that shocking will of your mother's.'

Tory, whose mind was drifting back to wondering in which quadrant of the car park she'd left her car, began to pay attention. 'Shocking?'

'I'd say so, wouldn't you? To raise two girls, and then at the last minute change your will to leave all your estate to one, and pretty well nothing to the other?'

'Pretty well nothing?'

Mrs Deloy's eyes widened. 'Oh, Tory. You did know? Surely you knew?'

Now Tory felt even more irritable about the sudden encounter. 'Surely knew what?'

'About the will! About the fact that your mother left a good deal more to you than she left to your sister.'

Tory was mystified. 'I'm sure that's not the case. Mum never would have done that.'

'But she did.'

'You read the will?'

'I didn't read it, Tory. I was bullied into witnessing it by that solicitor. But I had heard the two of them discussing it the day before, and I distinctly heard your mother saying she wanted to leave a good deal more money to you.'

'You heard Mum saying that?'

'I wasn't eavesdropping! I never pry into my families' affairs. It's just that as I was going into the kitchen to put on my pinny, I overheard that Mrs Hatcher ask if the extra was supposed to go to Megan Elizabeth or to Victoria Ann. Your mother definitely said "Victoria Ann".'

'Why would she ever have done that?'

'I don't know, Tory. But she did.'

Tory said somewhat accusingly, 'She talked to you quite a lot. You worked for her for years. You must have some idea.'

Mrs Deloy looked uneasy. 'Tory, it really isn't for me to say. But I will tell you that, after one of your visits, she began to fret about her will. She wasn't thinking straight by then, of course. She was confused by all those painkillers. But one day when I tidied up her room I found the weirdest list of figures—'

'Figures?'

'You know. Amounts of money. Money for plumbing bills and a lawn mower, somebody's skiing trip, something to do with jojoba – oh, there were loads of things. It just went on and on, all down the page. It was the weirdest writing. Not like your mother's steady hand at all. The letters were all straggly, and some of the words were spelt wrong, or broken off before the end.'

Tory stood waiting as Coral Deloy pushed on with the story she had told herself a hundred times was none of her business, never to be divulged. 'And, Tory, I think that she'd been trying to add up amounts. But all her columns had gone haywire. Noughts all over the place. Surely no lawn mower ever cost ten thousand pounds! I think your mother had been trying to even things up so that the pair of you would end up having had as much as one another, but she had got the answer to her sum completely wrong.'

Finally Tory grasped it. She burst out laughing. 'Mum didn't just get the wrong answer. She gave the extra wodge of loot to the wrong daughter!'

'No!'

'Yes.' Tory pulled a guilty face. 'I am the wasteful sinner who got the lawn mower and the jojoba and all that stuff. Poor Megan's never had a bean.'

'Tory!'

'It's true. Mum must have got completely mixed up in her head. Poor lamb.' She grinned at Mrs Deloy. 'Thank God you told me!'

'I was so worried, dear.'

'Of course you were!' Tory gave her a hug. 'You've done exactly the right thing by letting me know. Now I can put things right.'

Mrs Deloy could scarcely believe that her anxieties about that will she'd thought so wrong, yet witnessed, might now be laid to rest. 'Put things right? How will you do that?'

'Easy,' said Tory. 'First I'll explain to Megan exactly what happened. Then I'll send her a cheque for her fair share.'

*

Barry was most amused. 'My God! Old people! Don't they cause some trouble!'

'Be fair,' said Tory. 'It was the painkillers. Mum wasn't in the least addled up till the last few weeks.'

'It still doesn't explain your sister's state of mind. From what we saw, it was the ashes being thrown into the grave that set her off.'

'I know. But I can use it as an excuse to get in touch with her. And then maybe, if I offer a few placatory words about what Ned did at the funeral…'

'What? Tiresome boy. Ignoring the strictest orders…'

'Everyone very tense. A painful day, etcetera…'

'Yes, that should do it. What about the money?'

'What do you mean?'

Barry gave what he hoped looked like a casual shrug. 'You don't mind?'

'Giving half of it away?'

'It's not half any more. We've spent a massive amount in the last weeks. It is a hefty chunk of what is left.'

'Oh, well.'

He stared at her. 'That's all you have to say? "Oh, well?"?'

She gave him quite a telling look. 'So, tell me. Are you happier than you were before?'

He thought about it. 'Well, I love my car. It's a real beauty.'

Tory was scathing. 'A pity mine is crap and has to keep on going back.'

He said to her, 'Tory, you are amazing. You're really going to give your sister half of the estate?'

'If we have that much left.'

'I'll count it up tomorrow, but I'm sure we do.'

*

And they did. Just.

Tory rang Megan. 'This is a little difficult to explain…'

'I hope it's going to start with an apology.'

'Oh, fuck off, Megan,' Tory said. 'Just listen, will you? Mum got the will all wrong, and gave a great wodge more to me because she mixed us up.'

Megan had spent weeks telling herself how she'd react, should Tory ring. Frosty. Dismissive. Getting off the phone as soon as possible. But still she couldn't help but answer, 'What do you mean, "she mixed us up"?'

'It was the painkillers. They made her daffy-brained. She meant to give you loads more money to make up for all that Gordon gave us. But she told the solicitor the wrong name.'

Megan knocked off the frigid sister act. 'You're joking!'

'No, I'm not. We owe you an enormous amount of money. I'm going to have to do the sums and sort it out.'

There was a pause. Then, 'Don't bother,' Megan said.

'Sorry?'

'I said, don't bother.'

'Megan—'

'I just don't want it,' Megan interrupted her. 'I really, really do appreciate the fact that you're prepared to offer. And it is nice to know that Mum didn't turn nasty at the end, and it was all a mistake. But I've been getting on so well without—'

She broke off.

'Without the family?' Tory suggested after a moment's thought.

Megan's old habits of politeness triumphed. 'Well, not your family, of course.'

'Ours is the only family left.'

'Oh, dear. I suppose it is. Well, then, I mean, without the family money.'

'With all its psychic ties?'

'That's it!' Megan seized on the notion gratefully. 'Tory, I'm so glad that you understand. It's just I've realised that I can't be like you about money and stuff – all easy-come, easy-go. It matters to me.'

'Where it all comes from? Being fair and stuff? We always called you the Fair Do's Police.'

'You didn't!'

'Not to your face, of course.'

'I'd no idea.'

'Oh, you were terrible. Everything being equal was an obsession.'

'Was it? I suppose it was. Well, I am over that now. I won't say that I'm getting more like you. But I want to be free of having to think about anything like that ever again. I don't want any part of Gordon's money – not a single penny.'

'Well, tough!' said Tory. 'I don't want to walk around weighed down with guilt. So I'll be sending it to you in any case.'

'I shall just send it back.'

'Then I shall send it back to you again.' Remembering the last few ashes she'd dug into the grave around her forget-me-nots, Tory said merrily, 'I warn you, in these matters I have form.'

Megan caught the amusement in her sister's voice, but not the joke itself. 'Shall we have lunch?' she said. 'We could go to the bistro any day this week.'

'And this time I could pay.'

Now Megan, too, was laughing. 'Yes, this time, Tory, I will let you pay.'

15.

'You two are simply astonishing,' said Barry. 'One month you're sending your stepfather's charred remains back and forth to one another. The next, it's huge amounts of money.'

The uncashed cheque had come back yet again, this time disguised as something from the council. Tory stood looking at it. 'She's not going to win this battle.'

'What are you going to do this time? Stuff the thing down her bra as you come out of the bistro?'

'Oh, God! The bistro! I shall be late again.'

Tory snatched up her purse. She met her sister every Wednesday now, and she enjoyed it. Megan was turning into excellent company. And she was helpful. She had marched Tory to the garage and told the manager, 'You take this car in now and sort it out. Properly. And if my sister has to bring this lemon back another single time, she's going to sue.'

The car went into intensive care, and came back one week later. Since that day it had caused no trouble at all. Meanwhile, Megan had found a house. 'It's perfect for you! Not so near the school, but that won't matter long. You'll love it. And there's even a place for that enormous sofa.'

'Really? Because I had been thinking of getting rid of that.'

'Nonsense! It just needs all the covers laundering.'

'You can wash covers?'

'Tory! Why do you think that sofa cushions have zips?'

'Have they?'

'Yes. At the back.'

'I hadn't realised.'

And on and on. Malcolm took over Tory and Barry's investments. 'No, really. It's no trouble. All I'll be doing is mirroring my own.'

'Mirroring?'

'Doing what we do, so you don't have to think.'

'Well, that sounds easy enough.'

The only problem was the cheque, which just went back and forth. Once she had finally noticed it was out of date, Tory did rip it up and write another.

'Try using bank transfer for a change,' suggested Barry. 'You'll save a fortune on stamps.'

'Can't,' Tory said. 'She won't let on even which bank she uses, let alone an account number.'

'Cunning...' said Barry. 'Very, very cunning.'

And so the dance kept on till Tory cracked. 'All right. We'll keep the money. But, Megan, you must promise me that if you ever want your share of it, you'll say.'

'You will have spent it all by then.'

Probably true, thought Tory. She had suspected, even the last time she had stuffed it in an envelope, that it could probably not be fully honoured. 'Well,' she said, 'even if we have, we can still mortgage our lovely new house and pay you back.'

'Tory! There are to be no mortgages, no loans to other people and no more fancy cars! You two are just to carry on the way you did before, except that, thanks to Malcolm, you'll both have pensions.'

'All right,' said Tory meekly.

She'd only been in the new house four days before the doorbell rang. On the step was a cheerful-looking young man with a shock of brassy yellow hair. 'Hello,' he said. 'I'm Crispin. Megan sent me round. She said you'd need me. I'm a cleaning lady.'

'Are you?'

'I'm very good,' he said, as if he thought that she might doubt it. 'Can I please look around?'

Tory trailed him from room to room. 'I'd say five hours a week,' he told her at the end. 'But Megan thinks I might have to bung on an extra hour because of all the picking up.'

'The picking up?'

'She says—' He stopped, and then took off another way. 'She's worried that you won't have time to tidy up before I come, because of your new job.'

'What new job?'

'At the art gallery. Hasn't she told you?' He smiled seraphically. 'She's like that, isn't she? She sorts you out so fast, she doesn't always have the time to keep you up to speed with the plan.' He pulled out a chair and sat down at the new heat-proof table Megan had ordered Tory to buy. 'That's what she did to me – sorted me out from a great giant mess.'

'What sort of mess?'

Crispin turned cagey. 'Tell you another time. Let's start off with the full six hours, and see how it goes. Would you prefer me coming in when you're around, or when you're out.'

'When I'm out,' Tory said firmly. She felt so strongly about that, she said it over again. 'Definitely when I am out.'

*

The blow fell six months later. Everything was going swimmingly, and then the letter came. It was addressed to both of them. Barry got to it first because Tory was searching for the special fruit cake she'd hidden from Ned so Crispin (who'd turned out to be an academic whizz) would have something to sustain him while he was tutoring Lindy for exams.

'Blimey!' said Barry. 'I can't believe this letter says what I think it does.'

Tory was barely listening. 'Where did I hide that sodding cake? Where is it?'

'Look at this, Tory.'

'Not now. I have to find the fruit cake. Crispin must never get hungry.'

'I don't see why,' said Lou. 'I'm always starving before meals. And I live here.'

'He's in recovery,' Tory reminded Lou. 'He's on a plan called HALT. It stands for the rules that he's supposed to live by for the rest of his life. The poor lamb's never to allow himself to get too hungry, too angry, too lonely or too tired.'

'He got pissed off enough with Lindy last week when she hadn't done all the revision he set her.'

'Language!' Barry chided his younger daughter. 'Tory! You have to read this.'

'Found it!' She slammed the solid lump of fruit cake on the table and plumped herself down beside him. 'Oh, God! Not that lot. I had hoped that we'd never see that letterhead again.'

The letter was from Russell Powers Solicitors. She read it carefully from start to finish. 'Oh, Christ!' She read it through again. 'What are we going to do?'

Lou snatched the letter. She made a stab at reading through the first two paragraphs, and then complained, 'I just don't get it. What does it all mean?'

'It's a disaster!' said Tory. 'We've only just settled down. We have a lovely new house, two nice fat pensions, two dependable cars, a comfy sofa and a brilliant bloke who's ravelling up the pieces from Lindy's flaky educational past. Everything's tickety-boo. Life's pretty well perfect. Then this comes!'

'But what does it mean?' Lou asked again. 'Was it a mistake, all that money? Are Russell Powers going to take everything back?' The questions turned into a wail of anguish. 'Am I going to lose my lovely phone?'

'No,' Tory told her bitterly. 'You're probably going to get an even better one.'

For that was the sum of it. The letter said that Tory and Barry were the only living beneficiaries of the late Edith Iris Tallentire. Her principal beneficiary, Gordon Forsyth, had pre-deceased her. So since Victoria and Barry Challoner were the only others named in her will, they had inherited her money and a bank transfer would follow in due course.

Lou studied the look of exasperation on her mother's face. 'I just don't get it,' she complained. 'What is so awful about being given oodles more money?'

'Oh, you know nothing about life,' Tory reminded her.

'Da-ad?'

But he just shrugged.

'So who was Edith Iris Tallentire?' demanded Lou.

'She was your Grandpa Gordon's godmother.'

'His godmother? She must have been about a hundred!'

'She probably was,' said Tory. 'I certainly assumed that she died years ago.'

'But why did she leave money to you?'

'I don't know.' Tory shrugged. 'I do remember that your father and I did her a small favour once – something to do with a cow byre.' Recalling the details, she changed the subject for fear the children would learn something negative about the aunt and uncle who had been so helpful in the last few weeks. 'I never realised that she had no family. Or that she was so rich.'

Lindy had come into the kitchen. 'Crispin wants cake,' she told them before adding curiously, 'Who was so rich?'

'Some old bat called Miss Tallentire,' her sister told her.

Lindy reached for the fruit cake. 'Miss Tallentire? I would have thought that she'd have died ages ago. She must have been at least a hundred and ten the time I met her.'

Tory was startled. 'When did you ever meet her?'

'When Dad was in *The Pirate King* and Mum and Lou had flu so couldn't go. Grandpa took me and her. She was his godmother, he said, and I remember her name because he made me practise saying it all the way over in the car to pick her up. He said she was far too old-fashioned for first names, so I mustn't call her Ellen.'

'Edith,' corrected Tory.

'Whatever. So can I take this lump of cake up to Crispin?'

'Take a plate, too,' said Barry. 'And a knife.' He waited till Lindy was just out of hearing before he added, 'And tell him not to make too many crumbs or he might get too tired or too angry, clearing them up when he turns back into our cleaning lady.'

'Sssh!' Tory warned. 'You mustn't tease the boy.' Returning to the matter in hand, she stared at the letter again. 'Well, at least that explains it. You wore that beard all through *The Pirate King*. You might not have clocked that she was in the audience, but she must have recognised you when you came to her house to warn her about that cow byre business.'

'What cow byre business?' asked Lou.

They both ignored her. 'You think that's why she did it? Simply because we made an effort that time?'

'Why not? If she had no one else. She probably put us in her will for some small token amount. A little private joke. We've only got the whole shebang because Gordon died.' The very words 'the whole shebang' set Tory off again. 'Oh, God! What are we going to do?'

'If it's more money coming in,' insisted Lou, 'I don't see any problem.'

172

Her parents still ignored her. Barry read the letter once again. 'We could just give a chunk of it to charity,' he said, looking a little wistful. 'Then we could bung the rest into the bank, and just forget it.'

'Look at that bloody great amount!' said Tory. 'Banks don't leave you alone if you put even a fraction of that sort of loot anywhere near them. They're on at you the whole time – letters and phone calls. "You could do this, Mrs Challoner.", "Why don't you think of doing that?" No. It'd be a nightmare. And we've already used up weeks of Malcolm and Megan's time.'

Megan!

In a flash, the solution came. 'We'll give a chunk of it to charity, we'll keep a bit, and give the rest to Megan.'

'Oh, brilliant!' scoffed Barry. 'Here we go again. Cheques flying back and forth!'

'It won't be like that this time,' Tory said. 'It isn't Gordon's money, after all. I'll play the trump card of her children's legacies – the ones Mum snatched off them – then she can't mind. I'll put the screws on her until she feels she has to take it.'

*

It didn't take long. Megan buckled fairly soon. For one thing, she'd been feeling worse and worse about what she now thought of as Amy and Bethany's lost nest eggs. And for another, Malcolm was on her back. 'Tory's quite right, you know. This isn't money from Gordon. So you can take it without any fretting.' He gathered courage to say out loud what he believed that Megan – all of them really, except for him – must secretly be thinking. 'I'm just surprised Miss Tallentire left it to them, not you. After all, you were the one who lived next door, and took cakes round, and went to see her in the nursing home until she vanished into that other place.'

Megan was down to scraping the barrel for possible explanations. 'Maybe the solicitors who work at Russell Powers do such sloppy work that there was a mix-up of names in her will, just as there was in Mum's.'

'Maybe,' he said, though he knew better. Miss Tallentire had sussed him out. He knew that from what Elinor had said. But why she chose to leave her fortune to Tory and Barry was a total mystery – unless she thought that he and Megan had been in cahoots about the little scam, and

173

felt the urge to rub both their noses in it. As far as Malcolm knew, Miss Tallentire had never even met Tory or Barry, though she'd have known of their existence from Gordon.

That must be it.

Oh, well. All water under the bridge now. Here was the brand new cheque (written and signed by Tory) in his wife's hand. 'You're going to cash in this one, then?'

'I think I am, yes. And I'm going to turn it into investments for Amy and Bethany.'

'Quite right.'

'I think that I'd feel better if the girls weren't out of pocket.'

'Split that lot between them, and they'll be doing better than they would if they'd been given the original legacies.'

The notion of her family benefiting more than they would at the start made Megan somewhat anxious. She tried to console herself. 'Not that much better.'

'No,' he said hastily. 'Not that much better. Just about right, in fact.'

Megan gave him a grateful look. 'Yes. Just about right. Everything will have worked out fairly in the end.'

'And that's nice, isn't it?'

'Yes. Very nice.'

And what a massive relief, thought Malcolm. Who would have thought a quiet conversation with a golf chum could set off such a roller-coaster ride? The whole thing had been like that old-fashioned board game, *Bagatelle*, where the hard silver ball shoots out and ricochets from one side to the other till it falls in its final slot.

A very lucky slot this time, in his opinion. Everyone was happy now. Exactly like the end of the that Barry acted in once, wearing the most extraordinary beard. What was it called? *The Pirate King*. Disaster after disaster, or so it seemed, till suddenly, by the most brilliant tricks of plotting, everything had fallen into place.

Because, by ironies of fate, wrongs had at last come right. He could forgive himself. Even his mother-in-law had ended up buried with both of her husbands. All's well that ends well, indeed.

The phone rang. It was Tory. She was inviting them to supper. 'Barry's made far too much of his speciality bean stew. Can you come round?'

No. There were limits. She might have set both of his daughters up for life, but he could not abide their awful meals. 'Oh, I'm so sorry,' he said. 'Amy has just passed an exam with such good marks that we're all going out to celebrate. Won't you come with us? We promised her we'd go to Forley's and we'd drink champagne.'

'Champagne?' said Tory. 'Oh, that sounds just the thing!'

Malcolm caught Megan's eye. He rolled his eyes and made the gesture of forking something heavy in his mouth. 'Ask her back here for supper,' Megan mouthed.

'And then come back for supper here.'

He watched his wife as she fled to the kitchen to start defrosting things. Oh, he was happy. Everyone was happy. How had that worked out? It wasn't normal, was it?

No. It wasn't normal. But it bloody ought to be.

*

Megan studied the list so neatly clipped with magnets to the freezer door. What should they have? Lasagne? Moussaka? Or maybe just that wonderful beef casserole she made for Christmas and they never ate. She had been saving that for an occasion. It never occurred to her that Tory and Barry's family might end up sharing it. They weren't exactly the gourmands she had imagined sitting across the table when she first slid the carefully sealed dish onto the top shelf.

But there again, it was a celebration. Champagne, and lots of the finest beef casserole she'd ever made.

Why not? The girls were set up. Barry was pleased with her. She hadn't compromised that strange decision that had calmed her soul. Everyone was happy now.

And Tory was her sister, after all.

Fair's fair. Yes. Fair is fair.

18398004R00099

Printed in Great Britain
by Amazon